I can't

tell him.

Roxanne's desertion would be devastating, all the more so because it would be so public. If only there were more time. If only all those people weren't already out there. If only she could tell David in private, and they could concoct a face-saving story.

How different things would be if she were the one getting ready to marry David instead of her twin, Roxanne.

It should be me.

In the mirror across the room, Rachel caught sight of Roxanne's wedding dress hanging next to the mirror. And suddenly, she knew what she must do.

Dear Reader,

As the long summer stretches before us, July sizzles with an enticing Special Edition lineup!

We begin with this month's THAT SPECIAL WOMAN! title brought to you by the wonderful Jennifer Greene. She concludes her STANFORD SISTERS series with *The 200% Wife*—an engaging story about one woman's quest to be the very best at everything, most especially love.

If you delight in marriage-of-convenience stories that evolve into unexpected love, be sure to check out *Mail-Order Matty* by Emilie Richards, book one in our FROM BUD TO BLOSSOM theme series. Written by four popular authors, this brand-new series contains magical love stories that bring change to the characters' lives when they least expect it.

Pull out your handkerchiefs, because we have a three-hankie Special Edition novel that will touch you unlike any of the stories you've experienced before. *Nothing Short of a Miracle* by Patricia Thayer is a poignant story about a resilient woman, a devoted father and a cherished son who yearn for a miracle—and learn to trust in the wondrous power of love.

If absorbing amnesia stories are your forte, be sure to check out *Forgotten Fiancée* by Lucy Gordon. Or perhaps you can't pass up an engrossing family drama with a seductive twist. Then don't miss out on *The Ready-Made Family* by Laurie Paige. Finally, we wrap up a month of irresistible romance when one love-smitten heroine impulsively poses as her twin sister and marries the man of her dreams in *Substitute Bride* by Trisha Alexander.

An entire summer of romance is just beginning to unfold at Special Edition! I hope you enjoy each and every story to come!

Sincerely,

Tara Gavin,
Senior Editor

Please address questions and book requests to:
Silhouette Reader Service
U.S.: 3010 Walden Ave., P.O. Box 1325, Buffalo, NY 14269
Canadian: P.O. Box 609, Fort Erie, Ont. L2A 5X3

TRISHA ALEXANDER

SUBSTITUTE BRIDE

Silhouette®

SPECIAL EDITION®

Published by Silhouette Books
America's Publisher of Contemporary Romance

A huge "thank-you" to my wonderful editor, Gail Chasan, who has been with me through fifteen books and who I hope will be with me for many more to come. You're the best!

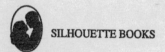

SILHOUETTE BOOKS

ISBN 0-373-24115-1

SUBSTITUTE BRIDE

This edition published by arrangement with Harlequin Books S.A.

Printed in U.S.A.

Books by Trisha Alexander

Silhouette Special Edition

Cinderella Girl #640
When Somebody Loves You #748
When Somebody Needs You #784
Mother of the Groom #801
When Somebody Wants You #822
Here Comes the Groom #845
Say You Love Me #875
What Will the Children Think? #906
Let's Make It Legal #924
The Real Elizabeth Hollister... #940
The Girl Next Door #965
This Child Is Mine #989
**A Bride for Luke* #1024
**A Bride for John* #1047
**A Baby for Rebecca* #1070
Stop the Wedding! #1097
Substitute Bride #1115

*Three Brides and a Baby

TRISHA ALEXANDER

has had a lifelong love affair with books and has always wanted to be a writer. She also loves cats, movies, the ocean, music, Broadway shows, cooking, traveling, being with her family and friends, Cajun food, "Calvin and Hobbes" and getting mail. Trisha and her husband have three grown children, three adorable grandchildren and live in Houston, Texas. Trisha loves to hear from readers. You can write to her at P.O. Box 441603, Houston, TX 77244-1603.

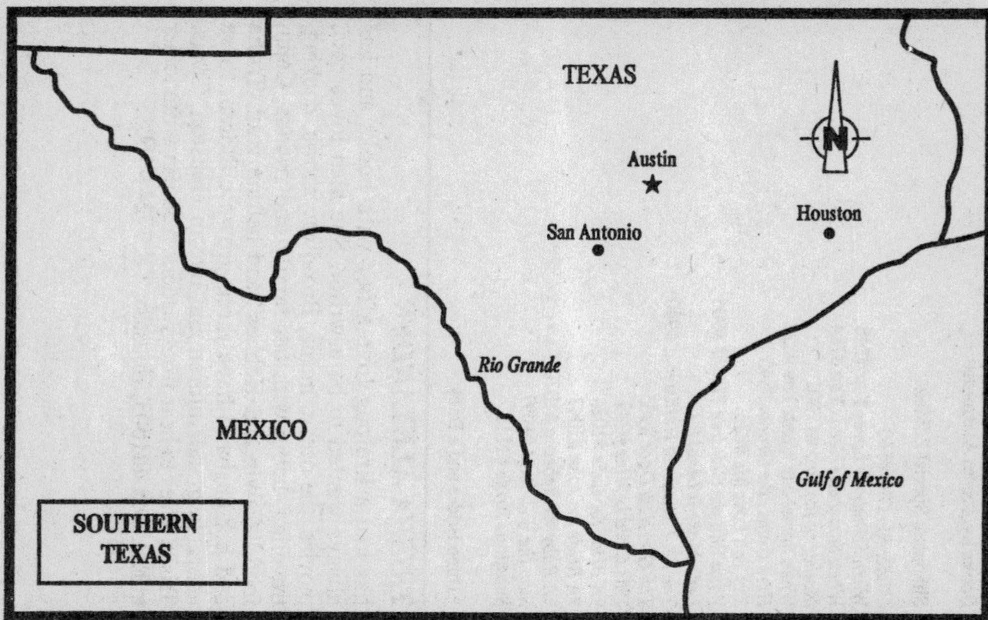
TEXAS
Austin
San Antonio
Houston
N
Rio Grande
MEXICO
Gulf of Mexico
SOUTHERN
TEXAS

Prologue

"Hey, David, Rachel, c'*mon!* What're you *doing?*"

Rachel Carlton looked up to see her twin sister, Roxanne, standing in the shallows, water fizzing around her bare brown feet. Behind her, the August sun glittered off the waters of the Gulf of Mexico, causing the surface to look as if it had been dusted with diamonds, and turning Roxanne's brown pigtails into spokes of gold.

"Come *on!*" Roxanne yelled again. She stood there, hands planted on her hips, feet splayed apart, obviously annoyed.

"We're building a sand castle," Rachel called, the note of apology automatic.

David Hanson, who, at twelve, was two years older

than the twins, abandoned the turret he'd been fashioning and stood. "We're coming," he called.

"Well, hurry *up.*" Roxanne turned and ran back into the surf.

David watched her, a smile of admiration tugging at the corners of his mouth as she dived fearlessly into an oncoming wave. Seeing the smile, something painful pinched at Rachel's heart.

Roxanne could always make David smile.

Roxanne could always make everybody smile, even when she was doing something she shouldn't be doing, which was most of the time.

Rachel, on the other hand, seemed to produce only frowns of impatience or, at the most, shrugs of tolerance.

"Let's go," David said, his dark brown eyes continuing to watch Roxanne as she cavorted in the surf. "We can finish the sand castle later."

Rachel looked down. "That's okay. You go."

He needed no further encouragement. The words were barely out of her mouth before he was racing across the dunes toward Roxanne.

Now it was Rachel's turn to watch, her blue eyes filled with a barely acknowledged yearning. This was the way it always was. No matter what David might be doing, if Roxanne called, he went. Rachel couldn't count the number of times he had completely forgotten everything...especially her.

But why shouldn't he? she thought with resignation. Although she and Roxanne were identical twins—so identical, in fact, that even their father had a difficult time telling them apart—they were nothing alike inside.

Roxanne was exactly like their father, daring and brave, always ready for the next adventure, always looking for a new challenge. She plunged headlong into life, unafraid of anything or anyone.

Rachel took after their mother. She was cautious and thoughtful. She rarely took risks, and when she did, it was usually because Roxanne had goaded her into it.

No wonder people preferred to be around Roxanne, Rachel thought sadly. If she'd had to choose between the two of them, she'd have chosen her sister, too.

Sighing, Rachel cast one final look of longing at the half-finished castle, then she slowly walked to the water's edge.

Chapter One

Eighteen years later

"And when David calls, say I'm sick—no, say I had a terrible headache and I'm sleeping and you don't want to disturb me. Okay?"

Rachel stared at her twin. "Roxanne, I really don't think—"

"C'mon, Rachel, what's the big deal?" Roxanne zipped up her black miniskirt and smoothed it down over her hips. Then she turned to look at herself in the cheval glass mirror. "*Yesss,*" she said, a satisfied smile playing around her mouth as she pivoted to look at all sides.

Rachel studied her thoughtfully. Roxanne, as always, looked terrific. Her shoulder-length golden brown hair, recently permed and styled in the breezy curls Rachel had adopted earlier that year, framed her face like a bright halo. Rachel still fought feelings of resentment every time she thought about Roxanne's hair. Why was it that no matter what Rachel did or how she tried to assert her independence, she was never allowed to have anything of her own?

Telling herself the hairstyle wasn't important, she continued to study her sister, who was still admiring herself in the mirror. In fashionable, chunky black heels, with the short skirt and lacy white shell topping it, her rounded breasts, small waist and long legs were shown to advantage.

But it wouldn't have mattered what Roxanne was wearing, Rachel thought with resignation. She could be in old jeans and a beat-up T-shirt, with no makeup on, and she would still turn heads.

She always turned heads.

"Please, Rach. It's just a little white lie..." Roxanne wheedled.

Rachel hardened her heart. "It's not a little white lie." No matter how much she loved Roxanne, what her sister was asking was wrong. "It's a huge, horrible lie. You're engaged. Your wedding is less than two weeks away. I—I don't know how you can do this to David."

Roxanne walked over to the bed where Rachel sat watching her, and took her hands. "Please, sweetie, please do this for me.'' Her dark blue eyes were earnest, imploring. ''It's not like you haven't done it before.'' Her smile was intimate—a reminder of all the times Rachel had filled in for Roxanne when Roxanne hadn't wanted to do something, of all the times they'd covered for each other and stood up for each other, of all the shared secrets....

''Don't remind me.'' Rachel wasn't proud of the times she'd aided and abetted Roxanne in her deceptions. But mostly, the things they'd done in the past were harmless pranks. This wasn't.

''If you'll cover for me with David just this one last time, I swear, I'll never, ever ask you again,'' Roxanne cajoled.

Rachel stubbornly shook her head.

Abruptly, Roxanne shrugged and dropped Rachel's hands. ''Okay, fine,'' she said breezily. ''*Don't* help me. When David calls, tell him whatever you like. I really don't care. I'm going out, anyway.''

''But Roxanne, I just think—''

''That's your trouble. You think too much. You've got to learn to *live.* Go for the gusto. Grab the brass ring. Be *daring.*''

''No matter who you hurt?''

Roxanne sighed dramatically. ''Oh, honestly, Rach, you're hopeless. What David doesn't know won't hurt him, and he'll never know about this.'' Then, seeing the unhappiness clouding Rachel's eyes, her voice softened. ''Look, sweetie, I promise. After David and I are married, I will be the best little wife in the world.

I won't ever do anything remotely like this again. But right now I can't help myself. Carlos is so—'' she gave a little shiver ''—so exciting and romantic...and *sexy.* David is...well, you know...David.''

Rachel thought David was exciting and romantic and sexy. She'd always thought so, ever since she'd been old enough to appreciate those qualities. ''David is wonderful,'' she answered quietly. ''You're lucky to have him.''

Roxanne grimaced. ''Oh, you just don't *understand.* If you were the one who was going to be tied down for the rest of your life, you'd feel the same way I do.''

No, Rachel didn't understand. She would never understand. Because if she were engaged to David Hanson, she would be the happiest woman in Houston. The happiest woman in the universe. He would be all she would ever need or want to make her life complete.

''I'm not telling him you're asleep,'' she finally said. ''I'll tell him you went out and...and I don't know where. You can figure out what you're going to say when he asks you about it.''

Roxanne smiled happily, then bent over and kissed Rachel on the cheek. ''Thanks, sweetie. Love you.'' She grabbed her purse, waved goodbye and started out the door. Then she stopped. ''Oops. Better not wear this.'' Tugging off the big, square-cut diamond ring gracing her left hand, she carelessly tossed it on top of her dresser. Then she waved again and left.

Rachel sat for a moment longer, but when she heard Roxanne's car backing out of the garage, she stood and walked over to the dresser. Lifting the ring, she stared at it for a long moment, then slowly slipped it on. She touched it lovingly. If this ring belonged to her, she would never remove it. Never.

Closing her eyes against the ache surrounding her heart, she prayed David wouldn't call tonight. She did not want to be an accessory in this subterfuge. David didn't deserve to be treated this way. He was so good, so sweet, so thoughtful and caring. He was *perfect,* and how Roxanne could think this Carlos Terraza could possibly be more appealing than David was beyond Rachel.

The trouble had all started three weeks earlier. It was a Friday night and David was away on a business trip, due back the next morning. The Carltons had been invited to a reception at the Mexican consulate, but Wylie Carlton, the twins' father, had another commitment, and Rachel had a bad cold and didn't feel like going out. Roxanne, never one to twiddle her thumbs, saw no reason why she shouldn't go alone.

There she'd met Carlos Terraza, an attaché posted to the consulate, and ever since, she'd spent every possible moment with him. Rachel wasn't sure what she'd been telling David, but she knew Roxanne hadn't seen him in several days. Rachel suspected Roxanne was sleeping with Carlos, even though Roxanne had not said so and Rachel hadn't asked.

Rachel didn't want to know. The more she knew, the guiltier she would feel.

What was *wrong* with Roxanne? Why couldn't she be happy with David?

Rachel thought about what Roxanne had promised, how she'd be true to David once they were married. Would she be able to keep that promise? If, practically on the eve of their wedding, she couldn't stay away from another man, how was she magically going to change because she had a wedding ring on her finger?

What would David think if he knew?

Rachel swallowed.

Dear God.

She prayed he would never find out. Roxanne's betrayal would hurt him unbearably. David was the most honorable person Rachel knew. He had more integrity in his little finger than most people had in their entire bodies. Being lied to would have to be the most cutting of all wounds. It made Rachel sick to think about it.

Yet what could she do?

Feeling totally impotent, she told herself to forget about Roxanne and David. She had no control over either one of them, so what was the point in worrying? She remembered something her grandmother Tobin used to say when Rachel was little and worrying about something that might happen. "Don't borrow trouble, missy. Expect the best, and if you do, the best will probably happen."

Don't borrow trouble.

It was good advice then, and it was good advice now, Rachel told herself determinedly. She decided she would pour herself a glass of wine, put some soothing music on the CD player and soak in a hot bubble bath.

And she would not spend one more minute thinking about anything unpleasant.

David Hanson hung up the telephone and sighed wearily. He hated talking on the phone, and he particularly hated conference calls. Unfortunately, for the past hour he'd been a captive participant in an especially tension-filled conference call between him, his grandmother Georgina, his future father-in-law, Wylie Carlton, and Wylie's executive vice president, Helmut Braun. The topic of the extended conversation was the upcoming merger of Carlton Oil Company and Hanson Drilling, which would take place a week after David and Roxanne were married.

Sometimes David wondered if the only reason his grandmother and Wylie Carlton were so in favor of the match between him and Roxanne was the merger of the two powerful companies and the resultant jump in stock prices that they were sure would follow.

Thinking about the merger depressed him. Thinking about anything to do with the business depressed him. The problem was, he hated his job. He had never wanted to work in the family business. He had never been the least bit interested in oil exploration or anything connected to it.

It hadn't been so bad when, after graduate school, he'd worked in the field. At least then he'd been outdoors and the work was interesting. But ever since he'd returned to Houston almost two years ago to take his place in management, he'd spent his days in endless meetings and strategy sessions where no matter what the topic, the main focus was always how the company could increase profits and decrease costs.

Yet what could he have done differently? After the death of his parents, his grandmother had raised him. He was her heir and the only Hanson left. The company would be his some day, and his grandmother had been grooming him to take over since he was in his early teens.

How could he crush her hopes and tell her he didn't care about the company that his grandfather had built single-handedly? How could he say that what he really wanted to do was work with kids? That ideally, he would like to become a counselor and specialize in helping underprivileged kids—in particular, fatherless boys—because he felt he could make a difference in their lives. And because he knew what it was like to grow up without a father.

For years now, he'd dreamed of using some of the money he'd inherited from his parents to buy a small ranch somewhere in the hill country—a place where kids could go to learn about nature and working outdoors and being part of a team. A place where they could discover their own self-worth and build their own dreams and maybe, just maybe, gain the strength and determination to make those dreams come true.

But how could he tell his grandmother and his future father-in-law, not to mention his future wife, that he had no interest in the companies that fueled their every waking thought? That he wanted to drop out of the rat race and do something that they would consider totally unrealistic—a romantic pipe dream. But the bottom line was, even if he *could* see himself disappointing them, how could he ask Roxanne to give up the work she loved and the city that suited her so perfectly, to go off to the country with him and lead a life so different from anything she had ever known?

He couldn't.

That's why he was still here.

He knew he shouldn't complain. He knew he was fortunate, that there were thousands, probably millions of people in the world who would trade places with him in a heartbeat. But no matter how many times he told himself this, he couldn't help how he felt.

With a resigned grimace, he stood and stretched his cramped muscles. He glanced out the windows behind him, which faced west. The June sky was a bright, clear blue, and far below, rush-hour traffic jammed the downtown streets and freeways. Today the sight depressed him even more than it usually did. Gathering up his briefcase, he turned off his computer, closed up his office and headed for the parking garage.

Well, he thought, it might have been a hell of a day, but at least he had the evening to look forward to. He hadn't seen Roxanne all week, and he'd missed her. But along with the anticipation he felt was a kernel of disquiet.

He hoped she'd be content to stay in tonight. It would be nice to order a pizza or Chinese takeout and just sit outside and relax in the walled courtyard of the patio home he'd purchased two months earlier. But knowing Roxanne, she would probably want to go out to dinner. She loved being around people, and seemed to crave a constant diet of noise and lights and activity.

David frowned. Lately she'd seemed even more restless than usual, her entire body thrumming with nervous energy and an edginess that disturbed him.

Sometimes he wondered if he could make Roxanne happy. He hated having these negative thoughts, but they seemed to be coming more and more often lately.

He'd been telling himself that once they were married, she'd calm down. Her tension was probably just prewedding jitters. Or maybe it was sexual frustration. God knows, he'd felt enough of that himself.

Unlocking his four-wheel-drive Bronco, David thought about the past two years, remembering how he'd felt when he'd laid eyes on Roxanne again after not having seen her for so long. How the fascination she'd held for him when they were kids returned, and with it, a new, adult emotion that was a combination of love and desire. He'd wanted her almost immediately, but she'd held him off with an elusiveness that had almost driven him crazy.

She'd gone out with him when he asked her, but

she'd refused to be pinned down when he'd tried to talk about his feelings. And then one day, shocking him because he had almost given up hope, she'd suddenly accepted his proposal of marriage. But she still wouldn't let him make love to her. She'd said she wanted to wait until they were married. She'd said she felt waiting would give their eventual union more meaning.

How could he argue with that? Although it was tough to wait longer, he was pleased and proud that, despite her outer sophistication, down deep where it counted, she was old-fashioned.

So he had agreed.

But lately he'd been having doubts. Maybe it had been stupid on his part to have consented to wait. Maybe, if they were already lovers, Roxanne would be more satisfied and content. Maybe...

Aw, hell, it was too late to worry about that now. He resolutely pushed his doubts from his mind. In ten days Roxanne would be his wife, and then there would be no more waiting...for anything.

Rachel lay in the tub, bubbles up to her chin, head resting on a tub pillow, listening to Van Cliburn's magical fingers rippling through a Chopin waltz. Dotted around the raised platform surrounding the tub were half a dozen lighted candles in crystal candleholders.

She lifted her left hand and allowed the candlelight to play across the diamond ring on her ring finger. She had been unable to resist keeping it on for a while. Pretending, for just a short time, that she was the one engaged to David.

She closed her eyes.

Imagined herself wearing the exquisite lace wedding dress hanging in Roxanne's closet...the expectant hush just before the organ music began to play... walking slowly down the carpeted aisle of St. John's on her father's arm...the scent of roses drifting in the air...David waiting at the altar...their eyes meeting...his smile...

Suddenly, shattering her fantasy, the doorbell chimed.

"Oh, phooey!" She considered ignoring the visitor—she certainly wasn't expecting anyone—but like a ringing telephone, the doorbell demanded her attention.

Sighing, she stepped out of the tub, wrapped her head in a towel and her dripping body in her thick terry-cloth robe, and hurried out to the foyer of the town house she shared with her twin.

She peered out of the peephole. Her heart knocked against her rib cage. David! With suddenly shaking hands, she unlocked the door.

He smiled down at her. "Hi."

"Hi." Her heart was beating too fast. It always beat too fast when she saw David. She self-consciously gripped the folds of her robe together. "C'mon in." As he followed her into the foyer, shutting the door behind him, she said, "I—I was taking a bath. That's why it took me so long to get to the door."

She clutched the folds of the robe tighter, acutely aware of her nakedness under it. Just as she was about to say that Roxanne wasn't home, he reached out and drew her into his arms.

"Are we alone?" he murmured, smiling down into her eyes.

"Y-yes, but—"

"That's good." Then, before she had a chance to even think, he lowered his mouth to hers.

The kiss was hot and possessive—a lover's kiss. Rachel's head spun as first shock, then desire banished all rational thought. She melted against him, years of silent love and yearning pouring into her response. Sensations pummeled her. The warmth of his lips, the taste of his tongue, the hint of stubble on his chin, the strength of his arms, the pure maleness of his body hard against hers. Need arrowed through her.

It was only as he slowly broke the kiss that reality intruded, and with it a rush of pure panic. *Oh, dear Lord! What have I done? What am I going to say? He thinks I'm Roxanne.*

He leaned his forehead against hers. "God, Roxanne, I don't know if I can wait ten more days."

His voice was ragged. His hands slid lower, cupping her bottom and pulling her closer as his mouth trailed to the hollow of her throat.

She could feel his arousal against her, and her heart

hammered crazily. "D-David," she said. "W-wait. Stop."

With all the willpower Rachel possessed, she managed to extricate herself from his arms. It was only then that she saw the ring, sparkling brilliantly under the lights of the chandelier.

Good heavens.

No wonder there'd been no question in his mind about her identity. In the past, if he wasn't sure who was who, he would say Roxanne's name, and if it was Rachel, she would smile and correct him.

Shame radiated through her, and Rachel couldn't meet his eyes. How could she tell him now that he'd been mistaken, that she was really Rachel? How could she possibly justify her actions?

Oh, no...

What would he think of her? And how was she going to be able to face him in the future? The knowledge that she was wearing Roxanne's ring pounded through her brain. What possible excuse could she give for that damning fact?

In that moment Rachel wanted the floor to open up and swallow her.

"Roxanne...you're upset," he said, his voice gentle. He reached for Rachel's hand, the one wearing his ring.

Rachel's heart beat furiously as she raised her eyes to his. She saw consternation and tenderness, apology and love. She knew, in that moment, that she would rather die than tell him the truth, because if he knew the truth, he would eventually figure out the reason behind her behavior. And then his dark eyes would be filled with pity, and she would have to live the rest of her life knowing he felt sorry for her.

"No, I'm not upset," she managed to say in a voice that sounded almost normal, almost calm. "It—it's just that I don't feel well. I think I have a fever."

Concern immediately clouded his eyes, and he cursed softly. "I should be shot, practically mauling you when you're sick. I'm sorry."

"Don't be silly, David," she said, using the tone of voice Roxanne would have used. "How could you know?"

He put his arms around her again, but this time he held her loosely. He kissed her forehead. "You *do* feel kind of hot. Have you taken anything?"

Of course she felt hot. She was hot with shame and humiliation. Hot with guilt.

Hot with desire.

"Not yet. But I'm planning to, and then I'm planning to go to bed and stay there."

He kissed her forehead again. "Good. You do that. And I'll call you in the morning." He pulled back a little and smiled down at her. "Do you have any sessions tomorrow?"

"Only one, but I can cancel it if I have to."

Roxanne was a fashion consultant who contracted with companies to hold seminars and workshops for their employees, where she advised them on their wardrobes and makeup. Earlier, Roxanne had told Rachel about tomorrow's schedule. Thank God, Rachel thought.

"Okay. Well, get a good night's sleep, sweetheart." He tipped her chin up and kissed her lightly. "I love you," he whispered.

"Oh, David." She was ridiculously close to tears. "I love you, too." *If you only knew...*

He gave her another hug, and then he was gone.

The moment the door closed behind him, Rachel began to tremble. She staggered back to her bedroom, threw herself across the bed and burst into tears.

Chapter Two

David whistled all the way home. The niggling doubt he'd felt on his way to Roxanne's house had disappeared in the wake of her eager and passionate response to him tonight.

His body stirred in remembrance.

What an idiot he was. Obviously, Roxanne wanted him just as much as he wanted her, and tonight, because she wasn't feeling well and her defenses were down, she'd shown him her desire in a completely satisfying way.

He smiled.

Everything was going to be all right. In fact, once they were married, everything—at least, everything concerning their relationship—was going to be great.

He'd been worrying for nothing.

And who knew, maybe someday he'd even be able to talk to her about his dream.

Rachel knew she had to tell Roxanne about what had happened, before Roxanne talked to David again. So she waited up until her sister got home. Even though it was after two in the morning, Rachel had no problem staying awake. She was still too upset with herself and too ashamed of her actions to be able to sleep.

Every time she thought about her abandoned response to David's kiss, she wanted to crawl into a hole and stay there forever. Her only comfort was in knowing that he'd had no idea she wasn't Roxanne.

The moment she heard the garage door going up she walked downstairs and out to the kitchen. A few minutes later, the door that led directly from the kitchen to the garage opened.

Roxanne, hair tousled, eyes dreamy and lips bare of lipstick and swollen from kissing, walked in. Her eyes widened. "Rach? Why are you still up? Is something wrong?"

Rachel swallowed. She had rehearsed what she would say. "No. Nothing's wrong. But something did happen tonight." At Roxanne's expression of alarm, Rachel hurriedly added, "It's nothing bad. Just something you need to know about before you talk to David again."

Roxanne dumped her purse and car keys on the kitchen table. She sighed. "What now?"

"Well...I was taking a bath...and the doorbell rang." Rachel kept her gaze steady, her tone casual. Above all, she did not want Roxanne to know how disturbed she was. "It was David."

"So?"

"He, um, mistook me for you." She managed a chuckle and was proud of herself.

Roxanne laughed. "What else is new? He's always getting us mixed up."

"I know, but this time, before I could tell him otherwise, he kissed me and, well, to tell you the truth, I was so flabbergasted, I let him. And then it just seemed easier somehow to keep pretending I was you. You know, less embarrassing all the way around. Anyway, I said I wasn't feeling well and planned to spend the evening in bed," she finished in a rush. "I just wanted you to know, because he plans to call you in the morning to see how you're feeling, and I didn't want you to be blindsided."

Roxanne smiled wryly. "He kissed you, huh? And he still thought you were me?"

"Yes." Rachel couldn't believe it. Roxanne wasn't upset. In fact, she seemed amused. If it had been Rachel, and Roxanne had confessed to kissing *her* fiancé, she'd have been upset.

More than upset.

She'd have been jealous.

Suddenly Rachel knew that her worries about Roxanne and her attitude toward David and their impending marriage were not silly. There was a serious problem here. A very serious problem.

Roxanne sank into one of the kitchen chairs. Her smile slowly faded, and suddenly her eyes were filled with torment. "Oh, God, Rach. What a mess my life is in. And this episode with David tonight, it only proves what I've been thinking for a long time. I mean, if he couldn't tell the difference between us when he kissed you, doesn't that say something about our relationship?"

Many times during the past hours Rachel had wondered the same thing.

Roxanne put her head in her hands. "I don't know what to do," she said in a muffled voice.

Rachel sat down, too, scooting her chair close to her sister's. She touched Roxanne's shoulder. "Roxie, look at me."

Roxanne lowered her hands. Her troubled eyes met Rachel's.

"Do you love David?" Rachel asked gently.

Roxanne nodded slowly. "Yes."

"Then why don't you stop this? Tell this Carlos person to get lost."

"I know that's what I should do, but I—I just can't seem to make myself."

"But honey, if you love David..."

"That's the trouble." Roxanne's voice sounded sadder than Rachel had ever heard it. "I do love him...but I've...recently I've come to realize I'm not *in* love with him. I guess I've been afraid to admit it to myself. I knew something wasn't right because I..." She hesitated. "I didn't *want* him, you know, physically. I kept telling myself that after we were married, it would be better. But now I know that's not true. Meeting Carlos, and the way I feel about him..." She swallowed. "The way I *want* him...it's changed everything."

The words hovered in the air around them.

Rachel took a deep breath. "If that's true, you've got to tell David. Before it's too late."

"Oh, God," Roxanne moaned. "How can I? Daddy will kill me. You know he has his heart set on this marriage. In fact, that's the whole reason I got engaged to David in the first place. I realize that now. I knew how Daddy felt. Shoot, he *told* me how he felt. He said he knew David wanted to marry me and how nothing would make him happier, and, I don't know, there was David pressuring me on one side and Daddy on the other, and it just seemed easier to go along with them."

Rachel's tender heart filled with pity. She could understand how, even in something as important as this, Roxanne could bend to their father's will. Wylie Carlton *did* have his heart set on this marriage. David Hanson was the closest thing to a son he'd ever have, and what better way of insuring the future of his family and his business than by having David marry his daughter?

And not just *any* daughter, either, Rachel thought

with a trace of bitterness. Oh, no. Wylie Carlton wanted David to marry Roxanne because Wylie thought the sun rose and set on Roxanne's head. According to their father, Roxanne was a chip off the old block.

"She's fearless, just like her daddy," he'd bragged more times than Rachel could count, his blue eyes glowing with pride.

The sisters stared at each other. "There's no way out," Roxanne said, tears glistening in her eyes.

"Until the minister pronounces you husband and wife, there's *always* a way out. I mean, I know it would be hard to tell David...and Daddy...but the alternative is worse. Isn't it?" She squeezed Roxanne's hand again. "Roxie, you've always been so brave. You can do this."

"I can't," Roxanne whispered. "I just can't."

Rachel worried half the night. Part of her hurt for Roxanne, but the other part, the part that Rachel tried to pretend didn't exist, wanted to throttle her sister.

Why had Roxanne allowed things to go this far, anyway? *You know why. Roxanne* has *to be number one in Daddy's eyes. She knew this was what he wanted, and there was no way she was going to disappoint him.*

If only Rachel had been home at the time....

She would have been, if she'd had any idea David was coming home. But she hadn't. When she'd made her plans to study advanced watercolor techniques with Gaulier in Paris, David had been working in Saudi Arabia and was supposed to stay there another year. And by the time she'd found out he was being brought back to Houston to begin learning the management end of the company, it was too late. She was already on a year's sabbatical in Paris, and her teaching position at Ashford Academy had been filled with someone else. She couldn't go home.

Rachel sighed.

The rest was history. By the time her year was up and she'd returned to Houston, David and Roxanne were already an acknowledged couple, and by Christmas they were officially engaged and Wylie Carlton was ecstatic. Rachel had no choice but to pretend a happiness she did not feel.

Somehow she'd managed to get through the intervening months. Somehow she'd kept a smile on her face and said and done all the right things. Somehow she'd convinced herself that if David was happy and Roxanne was happy, she would be happy, too.

But Roxanne wasn't happy.

And if she married David, he wouldn't be happy, either. Because he wasn't stupid. It wouldn't take long for him to realize something was terribly wrong.

And then what?

The next morning Rachel wondered if she should try to talk to Roxanne again. But Roxanne's door was shut, and when Rachel tapped softly, there was no answer. And Rachel really couldn't stick around waiting for her sister to wake up. She had a nine-o'clock appointment with the owner of the Blythe Gallery, who was considering showing her work.

It was already eight-fifteen. Rachel had to leave, because this chance for a show at Blythe was important to her, and she certainly didn't want to be late.

So, telling herself Roxanne's problems could only be solved by Roxanne, Rachel headed toward the museum district. She arrived at the gallery, which was situated conveniently near the Contemporary Arts Museum on Montrose, fifteen minutes early, but that was all right.

Smoothing down the skirt of her oatmeal linen suit and straightening the short, fitted jacket, she opened the gleaming glass-and-chrome doors that led directly into the main gallery. A polished brunette in a short black dress sat behind a small antique desk in the corner. There was nothing on the desk top except a white phone and an appointment book. "Yes?" she said, flashing a brilliant smile. "May I help you?"

Rachel introduced herself. Another blinding smile later, the brunette—who'd introduced herself simply as "Vivian, Mr. Blythe's assistant"—picked up the phone and murmured something into it.

"Mr. Blythe will be with you in a few minutes," Vivian said.

While she waited, Rachel walked slowly around the main showroom and studied the paintings on the walls. They were all abstracts in shades of red and brown, painted by an artist whose name she recognized from recent articles in art magazines. He had been described as "up-and-coming" and "a brilliant new talent." Envy pricked at her. She wanted this, too—the validation of knowing that others admired her work and were willing to pay for the privilege of owning it.

It was funny, she thought. She loved teaching art to children. She would probably always want to teach, no matter how successful she might be with her own art. There was something very satisfying about introducing a child to the wonders of creating something with his or her own hands and imagination. But she also needed this other kind of recognition, and the need was all tied up in her feelings about herself and her father and her sister.

"Miss Carlton?"

Rachel turned. A tall, gaunt man with a pencil-thin mustache and thinning gray hair smiled at her.

"I'm Phillip Blythe," he said, walking forward and extending his hand. "Let's go back to my office."

Rachel followed him down a carpeted hallway to a small, sun-filled office that faced the side street. She declined his offer of coffee and sat in the indicated chair. He took a seat behind a cluttered desk. Rachel's heart was beating a bit too fast, and she told herself to calm down. *This isn't world peace,* she reminded herself. The worst thing that could happen here would be for him to decline to give her a show.

He fingered her portfolio. His gaze was thoughtful.

Rachel girded herself for disappointment, resolving to be gracious even if it killed her.

"I like your work," he said. "I like it very much."

Rachel flushed with pleasure. "Thank you."

"I can give you a show in September, if you can give me at least thirty suitable paintings by then. Otherwise, we'd have to wait until next spring, because the gallery is fully booked for the remainder of the year as well as January through March of next year."

September! So soon! Euphoria flooded her, and she had the almost uncontrollable urge to jump up and hug him. Somehow she restrained herself and instead did a quick mental calculation. She already had the eighteen paintings that had comprised the portfolio she'd submitted for Blythe's evaluation. And she had more than two months before school started in the fall. If she worked hard from now until then, she should easily be able to complete twelve additional paintings. "That should not be a problem," she said.

"That's what I wanted to hear."

They smiled at each other.

"Well," he said briskly. "Let's talk about specifics." For the next thirty minutes they discussed the particulars of the show and then worked out the details of the contract. "I'll have Vivian send you the contract by the end of the week," Blythe said, standing.

Rachel stood, too. Blythe escorted her to the front door, where they shook hands.

"Thank you so much, Mr. Blythe," Rachel said. "I'm really looking forward to working with you."

He smiled, and this time his smile was warm.

"Please, call me Phillip. And the pleasure is all mine. I have great hopes for you, my dear."

Rachel practically floated home. All her unhappiness over the episode with David had been forgotten, and she couldn't wait to share her news with Roxanne. It was only when she reached the town house that her euphoria dimmed somewhat and she was reminded of how unimportant her triumph might seem in the face of Roxanne's problems.

Maybe I shouldn't tell her.

She needn't have worried. Roxanne wasn't there. And although Rachel spent most of the day at home, sorting through her sketchbooks and leafing through her idea file, Roxanne didn't return until very late that night, by which time Rachel was already in bed and half asleep.

The next morning, when Roxanne finally came downstairs and Rachel got a good look at her sister's strained expression and the shadows under her eyes, she decided her good news could definitely wait. Somehow, being happy about the upcoming show seemed cruel when Roxanne was so miserable. Rachel knew her misgivings about telling Roxanne were ridiculous. It wasn't as if everything in Rachel's life was wonderful. She had her own hell to live with. After all, the man she loved was soon to marry someone else. But, of course, Roxanne didn't know that.

The excitement that had sustained Rachel for the

past twenty-four hours faded completely, and the old, familiar ache of longing threatened to overwhelm her.

In that moment a terrible foreboding seized her.

They were in such a mess.

No good could possibly come out of this impossible situation. Rachel knew, with a terrifying certainty, that sooner or later, something dreadful was going to happen.

It was only a matter of when.

By the time the day of the rehearsal dinner arrived, Rachel felt as if she'd been holding her breath for days. She got up at seven, taking care not to be too noisy. She knew Roxanne had been out very late the night before. She was afraid to know the reason.

Consequently, she was surprised to hear Roxanne coming down the steps twenty minutes later.

"You're up early," she said, turning to smile at her twin. The smile died on her lips. Roxanne's eyes were all puffy and red. She looked awful.

Rachel poured Roxanne a mugful of coffee and silently handed it to her. "Sit down," she said gently. "Tell me what's happened now."

Roxanne's face twisted. Her eyes filled with tears. "C-Carlos is leaving on Monday. H-he's going back to Mexico. I—I'll never see him again." The tears spilled over, rolling down her face.

Even though Rachel knew this was probably the best thing that could have happened, she couldn't help feeling compassion for her sister's distress. She walked over and put her arms around Roxanne, who buried her face against Rachel and cried as if her heart were breaking. Rachel held her and smoothed her hair and wondered what on earth was going to happen to all of them.

When Roxanne finally quieted, Rachel said, "Is Carlos leaving because of you?"

Roxanne sniffled. "Yes. He asked for reassignment. He said he couldn't stay here, not if I was going to marry someone else. He...he said he loves me, and the thought of me being with another man was too much."

In some strange way, knowing that Carlos cared for Roxanne, that this affair wasn't a casual thing with him, as Rachel had feared, made Rachel feel better.

"He wants me to go with him."

"Marry him, you mean?"

"Yes."

Rachel couldn't prevent the tiny spark of hope that ignited. "And...what did you tell him?"

"What *could* I tell him? I told him it was impossible. How can I go with him? How can I marry him? I mean, my wedding to *David* is tomorrow!" She sank into a chair. She looked completely drained, as if the life had been squeezed out of her.

For long moments, neither spoke. Then Roxanne sighed deeply. "I'm sorry. I shouldn't be dumping this on you. None of it is your problem."

"Don't be silly. Of course it is. Anything that affects you affects me, too. You know that. I just wish I could help."

Roxanne's attempt at a smile didn't quite make it. "You *have* helped. You've listened, and you haven't told me I'm a terrible person."

"That's because you're not a terrible person," Rachel said softly.

Roxanne's eyes filled with tears again. She angrily brushed them away. "Yes, I am. I'm a coward. If I wasn't, I'd tell Daddy and David the truth."

"It's not too late."

"Yes, it is. It was too late the day I accepted David's proposal, and you know it." She took a long, shaky breath and stood. "Well," she said with a false briskness, "it's not the end of the world, is it? I'll get over this. I've gotten over love affairs before. It's time to stop feeling sorry for myself and go back upstairs and try to get some sleep. Otherwise I'm gonna look like hell at the rehearsal tonight."

"Are you sure you're going to be okay?"

Roxanne shrugged, her eyes bleak. "I have to be, don't I?"

As soon as the dessert dishes were cleared away, Wylie Carlton stood and tapped his spoon against his crystal water goblet. The babble of voices from the attendees at the rehearsal dinner died down. Smiling faces looked his way expectantly.

When he was satisfied that he had everyone's attention, Wylie reached for his champagne flute. Raising it, he smiled across at Roxanne and David, who were seated on the other side of the round table.

"To Roxanne, my darlin' daughter," he announced in his usual booming voice, "and to David, who has always been like a son to me." He smiled happily. "Tomorrow's the day I've been waitin' for for years—the day that will mark the official merger of our two families."

"Hear, hear," someone said.

Wylie lifted his glass higher. "May you live a long and happy life together, and may you present me with lots of grandchildren!"

The guests laughed and drank the toast.

Rachel sipped her champagne and looked at Roxanne. She looked beautiful in her short black lace cocktail dress, and she was trying hard to act happy and normal. Too hard, Rachel thought. Her smile was brittle and there was an almost hectic glitter in her eyes. Was it only Rachel who saw the unhappiness and desperation behind them?

Her glance slid to David. What was he thinking? she wondered. Tenderness flooded her as she studied his beloved face. He wasn't classically handsome. His face was too long, his nose a bit too large, his features too strong. Despite these minor flaws—or perhaps because of them—he was enormously appealing.

His eyes were his best feature, she thought. They were a melting brown, the color of dark chocolate, and fringed by thick, curly dark lashes. His hair was almost black, and he always kept it cut short, because otherwise it curled too much, which he didn't like. He wasn't extremely tall, maybe five-eleven or so, but he seemed taller, maybe because he had a powerful build from his regular workouts. He had a deep, quiet voice and an endearing, almost shy smile.

He was also a really nice man, the kind of person who listened more than he talked and who always seemed interested in whatever you had to say.

He was, in a word, perfect.

He looked wonderful tonight in a beautifully cut charcoal pinstripe suit. Clothes looked good on David, and he liked dressing well. It was his one vice, Rachel had often teased.

As if he felt Rachel's eyes upon him, he turned and smiled at her. Rachel's heart turned over. She loved him so much. She smiled back, again wondering what he'd been thinking. Did he suspect a problem? Surely he realized Roxanne wasn't herself tonight. *Oh, David, why couldn't you have fallen in love with me?*

Just then David's grandmother, Georgina Hanson, stood to make her toast. Rachel shook off her melancholy and smiled fondly. She loved Georgina—almost as much as if she were her grandmother instead of just an old family friend. The older woman looked beautiful tonight, her petite figure and snowy hair complemented by a pale blue chiffon dress. She was wearing a necklace and earrings of sapphires and diamonds that Rachel knew were old family heirlooms that would probably be passed on to David's wife someday.

To Roxanne.

The thought brought a sharp stab of pain, and Rachel wondered if the day would ever come when she could think about Roxanne and David as husband and wife without the accompanying misery.

"I hope you will be as happy in your marriage as I was in mine," David's grandmother said, finishing her toast and pulling Rachel's attention away from her worries and back to the festivities. "I know if David's parents were alive today, they would be as happy as I am." Her smile was bittersweet. David's parents had died in a boating accident when he was only eight years old.

Again the guests drank.

Several others made toasts, including Hank Schermer, David's best man, who had flown in from Atlanta that morning. As he spoke, Rachel belatedly realized she should propose a toast, too. She quickly got to her feet when Hank was finished.

"To Roxanne, my sister and my best friend, and to David, who already seems like part of our family—I hope you'll be very happy." Her eyes met Roxanne's. *I mean it. I do love you. And even if you are marrying the man I love, I still hope you'll be happy.*

Their gazes clung for a moment, then Roxanne lifted her glass and quickly drained it.

Someone began hitting their water glass with a spoon, and soon the rest of the guests joined in, setting up a clamor.

"That means you have to kiss her," someone said.

David laughed and put his arms around Roxanne. He tipped her chin up.

Rachel couldn't look. She mumbled something about the ladies' room and escaped from the table as quickly as she could. When she reached the safety of the lavatory, she splashed cold water on her face, repaired her makeup and once more got herself under control.

Even so, she wasn't sure how much more she could take, so after returning to the private room where their party was being held, she headed straight for Roxanne and David.

"I'm not feeling great," she said, "so I think I'm going to go. Do you mind?"

"No, of course not," Roxanne said. She looked at David. "You know, I'm really tired myself, and tomorrow's a big day. Why don't I go with her? The party's about to break up, anyway."

"But I thought we'd—"

"That way you can visit with Hank," Roxanne continued, just as if he hadn't spoken. "I know you guys have things you want to talk about, and if I'm there, I'll cramp your style."

"No, you won't," David said.

Rachel wondered if Roxanne's eagerness to leave had anything to do with Carlos. She tried to catch Roxanne's eye, but Roxanne didn't look at her.

"Yes, I will." Roxanne stood. "I'm going to go say my goodbyes to everyone." Now she looked at Rachel. "Then we can go."

Before Rachel could reply or David could protest further, she'd already moved away.

David looked at Rachel.

Rachel shrugged. "Sorry."

He seemed about to say something, then stopped, got up, took her arm and walked her over to the corner, out of earshot of any of the others. Something about his expression made Rachel's stomach flutter in fear. She held her breath.

"There's something wrong with Roxanne," he said, "and I think you know what it is."

Chapter Three

Rachel's heart skipped. "Besides nervousness, you mean?" She didn't want to lie to him.

He nodded, his concerned gaze moving past Rachel. She knew he was watching Roxanne make her fare-wells. "She seems, I don't know...wired and weird. Like something's bothering her."

"I, um, don't know what to tell you," she hedged. "Have you *asked* her if anything's wrong?"

He shook his head.

"Well, don't you think you should ask *her* instead of me?"

He eyed her thoughtfully, while inside she squirmed.

Then he shrugged. "Yeah, I guess you're right.

She's the one I should be talking to.'' Frowning, he looked at Roxanne again.

It hurt Rachel to see the worry lines in his forehead. Honestly, this whole mess was so unfair to him, and he didn't deserve it. Once more, she wanted to throttle her sister. ''Listen, David, if you want to talk to her, I'll leave now and you can bring her home.''

For a moment he looked as if he were going to agree. Then, giving her an embarrassed smile, he said, ''Aw, hell. She said she was tired. And she *has* been working hard lately. I've hardly seen her.''

Guilt pricked Rachel, followed by a rush of anger. Why should *she* feel guilty? *She* hadn't done anything wrong.

Sure you did. You deceived David last week. And you're deceiving him now.

''I'm sorry,'' she said inadequately.

''Stop saying you're sorry. It's not your fault.'' He threw his arm around her shoulders. ''Thanks, Rach. You're a good friend. In fact, you're the best. Some guy's going to be awful lucky to get you.''

Oh, David, David... Rachel looked down, afraid the intense emotions battering her would show in her eyes. Why did she love him so much? Why couldn't she master this?

''Hey,'' he said softly. ''I didn't mean to embarrass you.''

Somehow Rachel managed to raise her eyes and smile at him. ''Thanks, David. That means a lot coming from you.''

* * *

An hour later both sisters were home and in their respective rooms. Rachel was already in bed, but she could hear Roxanne moving around. She wondered what her sister was thinking. They hadn't talked on the way home from the party. Roxanne had been lost in her thoughts, and Rachel was afraid of what she might say if she ever got started, so she'd been quiet, too.

They still hadn't talked when they reached the town house. Roxanne headed for the cupboard where they kept the aspirin. She downed two, then said wearily, "I'm going up to bed. See you in the morning."

Rachel just nodded. "Me, too."

Now Rachel wondered if she should have told Roxanne that David was worried. But what good would that have done? It wouldn't have changed a thing. Besides, the twins had exhausted the subject. Roxanne had made her decision. She was marrying David, as scheduled, so all Rachel could do now was hope for the best.

The sounds next door stopped, and Rachel knew Roxanne was in bed. She hoped her sister would be able to sleep. Rachel closed her own eyes. She needed sleep, too. Getting through tomorrow would take all her strength. She decided to count, very slowly, which sometimes helped her to relax. She had just gotten to thirty-four when she heard Roxanne's phone ring. It rang only once.

Rachel lay still, listening. Either the party had hung

up or Roxanne had answered. For a moment there was silence, and she relaxed. But then she caught a sound, followed by another.

Roxanne was talking to someone.

Maybe it's David. Maybe he called to say good-night.

She heard nothing further and had just decided it had indeed been David calling when a floorboard creaked. A few minutes later she heard soft footsteps going down the stairs, followed a few minutes after by the sound of the garage door opening.

That could mean only one thing. Roxanne was going out to meet Carlos. On the eve of her wedding, only hours before she would pledge herself to David, she was going out to be with another man.

David toed off his shoes, sighed gratefully and propped his feet on the coffee table. He and Hank had just gotten back from the rehearsal dinner and they had settled in David's living room. Even though David had been taken aback by Roxanne's suggestion that she go home with Rachel, now he realized how thoughtful it had been of her to give him this time with Hank, who had been his college roommate and was still his best friend. Tonight would probably be their only chance to talk.

"Well?" He looked at Hank expectantly. "What'd you think of her? Isn't she everything I said she was?"

Hank grinned. "Your grandmother? Yeah, she's a foxy lady, all right."

David picked up a pillow and threw it at Hank, who dodged it neatly. "You know who I meant."

Hank laughed. "Okay. You didn't exaggerate. She's gorgeous."

David smiled happily. "She is, isn't she?"

Hank nodded. "So is Rachel. Man, those two look so much alike. If they hadn't been dressed in different outfits, I wouldn't have been able to tell which one was which."

"I know. Half the time, even I can't tell them apart." David laughed again, remembering once when he'd nearly kissed Rachel, thinking she was Roxanne, and how Rachel had blushed when she'd realized his intention.

"Um, is Rachel going with anyone?"

The question was posed casually, almost as an afterthought, but David knew Hank well enough to understand that it wouldn't have been asked if Hank wasn't interested. "Not that I know of. Why? You interested?"

Hank shrugged, then, losing the battle to appear nonchalant, he grinned sheepishly. "Yeah, I think I am."

"And I suppose you want me to put in a good word for you."

"Hey, *buddy,* I figured you'd *want* to tell her what a great guy I am."

"So you want me to lie, then?"

Hank picked up the pillow David had thrown earlier, and David ducked. "Okay, okay, you twisted my arm," he said when they'd both finished laughing. "Tomorrow, first chance I get, I'll talk to her." But for some reason he didn't feel very enthusiastic about the prospect of Hank dating Rachel. Maybe it was because Hank had always played the field and, in the process, broken more than a few hearts.

The two fell silent for a moment, then Hank, frowning a little, said, "You know, if I hadn't known which twin you were engaged to, I would've guessed it was Rachel."

"Rachel? Why do you say that?"

"She just seems more your type. You know, quieter, more serious, more thoughtful."

David started to dispute this statement, then stopped. Hank was right. Rachel *was* more David's type. In fact, several times in recent months he'd had the guilty thought—quickly banished—that he wished Roxanne was a bit more like Rachel. The thought had disturbed him, because all his life he'd thought of Roxanne as perfect. "What can I say? Opposites attract."

Hank nodded, but his steady gaze made David squirm a little. To change the subject, he said, "Tell me how your job's going. Do you still like it?"

Hank worked in the publicity department for the Atlanta Braves. "Yes. It's great. Interesting and fun."

"Fun?" Envy tugged at David. "Work isn't supposed to be fun."

"Yes, it is. In fact, when it stops being fun, I'll find something else to do."

Now the envy was full-blown. "You're lucky, you know that?"

Hank studied him thoughtfully. "Still hate what you're doing?"

David shrugged. "It's not so bad."

"Hey, buddy, this is me, Hank, you're talking to."

David grimaced. The truth was, he lived for Friday night, and when Monday morning came, he dreaded going back. "I hate it," he finally said.

"Why don't you tell your grandmother how you feel?" Hank said after a bit.

"It's not that easy. You know how much she's counting on me taking over the company."

"Yeah, but who knows? Maybe, if she knew how you feel, she might surprise you."

The two of them had been over this ground before, and suddenly David was sorry he'd introduced the subject with his comments about Hank's job. He shrugged. "Maybe."

"I'm serious. Have you ever tried to talk to her about it?"

"No." That wasn't strictly true. David had tried, once, but either his grandmother wasn't really listening or she didn't want to hear what he had to say, for she'd neatly managed to steer the conversation into safer territory, and David had never tried again.

"I think you should," Hank said.

"Yeah, well, who knows. When Roxanne and I get back from our honeymoon, maybe I'll talk to her about it then." He forced a lighter tone. "Enough about my job. Tell me about Julie. What's she up to these days?'' Julie was Hank's younger sister and a favorite of David's.

Hank smiled fondly. ''She's got a new boyfriend, and it's looking serious.''

''Oh?''

They talked for another hour or so, getting caught up on each other's lives and the lives of mutual friends. Finally Hank yawned. ''I'm bushed. I've been up since five this morning. I think I'll hit the sack.''

David glanced at his watch. It was after one. He stood and stretched. ''Yeah, me, too. You know where everything is, don't you?''

Hank nodded and headed upstairs. David locked up, turned off the lights, then headed for his own bedroom.

Later, lying in bed, David thought about their conversation. He remembered Hank's remarks about Rachel and wondered what his friend would say if he knew that David's grandmother had said something similar to David when he'd first told her about his engagement. At the time, her statement that Rachel seemed more suited to him had stunned him, because it was so unexpected. It had also bothered him that his grandmother, whose opinion he respected and valued more than anyone else's, should question his choice. Before long, though, he'd realized Georgina Hanson didn't disapprove. She'd just been honestly surprised, and once she got used to the idea that it was Roxanne he loved, she was just as enthusiastic about the marriage as Wylie Carlton.

David punched up his pillow and looked out the window. The moon shone brightly in a cloudless sky, casting patterns of light across the room. Tonight was the last night he would sleep alone. Twelve hours from now he would be a married man and Roxanne would be sharing his bed and his life. It would be a good life, too, because despite his grandmother's and Hank's comments, David had made the right decision. Roxanne's devil-may-care approach to life would balance out his too-serious one. She would be good for him, and he would be good for her.

We'll have a great marriage, he reassured himself. *Everything will work out fine.* He was still telling himself that all would be well twenty minutes later, when he finally fell asleep.

Rachel didn't mention the fact that she'd heard Roxanne go out the night before, and Roxanne didn't say anything, either. In fact, Roxanne slept until nine, and by the time she'd showered and emerged from her room, it was almost ten and time for the arrival of the stylist who would be doing their hair and makeup.

Roxanne avoided Rachel's eyes as she poured herself coffee and then, turning her back to Rachel, she sipped at her coffee and stared out the window over the sink. A male cardinal landed gently on the lip of the bird feeder mounted on the sill, his scarlet plumage bright in the morning sun.

Rachel watched him as he fed and wondered what

Roxanne was thinking. "It's a beautiful day for a wedding," she murmured after a moment.

"Yes."

Their father had suggested holding the reception on the back lawn of the family home, saying he would have tents put up, but Roxanne had vetoed the idea, saying, "I don't want the guests sweating, Daddy. I want this to be an *elegant* wedding." As usual, Wylie had given in to Roxanne's wishes.

"I'm glad you decided against an outdoor reception, though."

Roxanne nodded, still not looking at Rachel.

Rachel started to say something else in the same vein, then thought how silly it was to pretend everything was normal. The two of them would have to spend most of the day pretending. Why not be honest with each other while they could? She walked over to her sister and gently squeezed her shoulder. "Roxie."

Roxanne slowly turned around. Her eyes were bleak as they met Rachel's.

"I just want you to know," Rachel said softly, "that no matter what, I love you, and I'll always be here for you."

Roxanne swallowed. Setting her mug down on the counter, she allowed herself to be drawn into Rachel's embrace. For a long moment they held each other. Then, slowly pulling away, Roxanne said, "I love you, too, and I don't know what I'd do without you."

Soon after, the stylist arrived, and from then on, they had no opportunity for private talk.

* * *

"I'm glad you decided against cutting your hair," Nina, the stylist, said as she finished fashioning Roxanne's hair into a sophisticated upsweep. "Longer hair looks better on a bride, I think, especially with the headdress you chose."

Roxanne's eyes, shadowed with pain, met Rachel's briefly. A few days earlier, she had said how much Carlos loved her hair and how he'd asked her not to cut it when she'd said she was considering it. Rachel couldn't help wondering if Roxanne would have made the same decision if it had been David who had voiced the objection. Immediately, she banished the thought. *Don't judge her,* she told herself. *It's easy to criticize someone else. Besides, you're not exactly unbiased, are you?*

When Nina finished with Roxanne, she turned to Rachel. "I think your hair should be worn up, too," she said.

"No, I don't think so," Rachel protested. "This is Roxanne's day. I don't want to take away—"

"I certainly don't mind," Roxanne interrupted. "And I agree with Nina. Your hat will look better if you wear your hair up."

The bridesmaids were wearing lacy aquamarine picture hats trimmed with pink satin ribbons and tiny pink rosettes to match their aquamarine taffeta dresses.

Rachel finally succumbed to Nina's and Roxanne's arguments and allowed the hairdresser to arrange her hair in an identical upsweep.

Afterward, Nina applied their makeup, and before they knew it, it was eleven-thirty and time to leave for the church. The wedding was scheduled for one o'clock, and the reception would start at two. Roxanne and David were booked on a seven-o'clock flight to Miami, where they would spend the night. Their final honeymoon destination was the Caribbean island of Colombé, and that flight would take place the following morning.

By noon, the sisters were ensconced in the bride's room at the church. The other bridesmaids were dressing at home and would be arriving separately. The wedding coordinator, after saying she would meet them in the vestibule after they were dressed, had gone out to check everything in the church.

Slowly the sisters undressed. Rachel wondered what Roxanne was thinking. Suddenly Rachel missed her mother desperately. If only her mother were alive, if only Rachel had her to confide in. But Jayne Carlton had been dead for fifteen years, a victim of breast cancer. And Rachel had no one to help her—or Roxanne—get through this day.

They began putting on their wedding finery. Rachel, clad in a strapless bra and filmy, floor-length half-slip, stepped into her satin pumps and reached for the aquamarine taffeta dress. Roxanne, similarly clad, reached for her shoes.

Just then, there was a knock at the door.

Both sisters looked up.

Rachel frowned. "It's probably Liz," she said, referring to the wedding coordinator. "Just a minute," she called out. Hurriedly donning her dress, she walked to the door and unlocked it.

Behind her, Roxanne stepped behind the screen provided for anyone who desired privacy when dressing or undressing.

Rachel opened the door.

Her eyes widened. Standing there was a handsome, dark-haired man who looked to be in his mid-thirties. For a brief moment she thought he was a delivery person of some sort, but one look at his designer slacks and shirt told her that couldn't be. Besides, he had nothing in his hands.

He smiled. "You must be Rachel."

Suddenly Rachel knew exactly who he was. Her heart sped up. *Oh, my God.*

"I am Carlos Terr—"

Before he could finish, Roxanne burst from behind the screen. With a glad cry, she flung herself into his arms. "Carlos! Oh, Carlos!"

"*Querido,*" he murmured, followed by a string of Spanish spoken so fast and so low, Rachel couldn't understand most of it.

The kiss he gave Roxanne, who eagerly accepted it, was so intimate, Rachel felt uncomfortable watching them. Stunned by his unexpected arrival, she stood there in a daze before the realization that the door was still open penetrated. Dear heaven! Anyone could walk past and see them. Walking behind them, she quickly closed it, her mind spinning with the possible ramifications of Carlos's presence.

"Roxanne," she said.

Slowly, reluctantly, Roxanne and Carlos drew apart, although he kept a protective arm around her. Roxanne seemed oblivious to her state of undress—she was still wearing only her white satin slip and undergarments—and she looked as dazed as Rachel felt.

"I—I thought you were gone," she said to Carlos. "I thought I'd never see you again."

"I couldn't go without you, my darling." He tipped her face up to his. "We belong together."

"But Carlos, I—"

"You don't love this David person. I know you don't. You love me." His voice throbbed with passion. "I'm not leaving without you."

Roxanne's throat worked, and a tear trembled at the corner of her eye.

Carlos gently wiped it away. "Do not be afraid to follow your heart, my love. Come away with me. Now, before it is too late."

Roxanne slowly turned, her blue eyes pleading for understanding as they met Rachel's. "I'm sorry," she whispered. "I...Carlos is right. I can't go through with this marriage."

Rachel just stared at her, shocked.

"Carlos," Roxanne said in a firmer voice. "Do you mind waiting outside? I—I need to talk to Rachel privately for a moment." When he seemed about to object, she stood on tiptoe and kissed him. "I'll join you in a couple of minutes, I promise."

When the door closed behind him, Rachel finally found her voice. "Roxanne, you can't do this. You can't! Not now. Not today. What...what about David? What about Daddy? What about all those people out there waiting for you?"

"You were the one who said it would be wrong to marry David if I didn't love him," Roxanne cried. She rolled her slip down and reached for the sundress she'd worn to the church.

"I know, but this...leaving him like this..." Words failed Rachel.

"I know it's awful. But love, real love, the kind of love Carlos and I have, it's so special and so wonderful and it...it doesn't come along every day. Some people are never lucky enough to find it. And when you do, you have to seize it." She slipped her feet into her sandals, then reached for Rachel's hands. "Besides, marrying David when I don't love him would be a much worse thing to do to him than I'm doing now. I'm only sorry I'm leaving this mess for you to clean up, but you'll think of something to tell everyone."

Rachel's mind was numb. Her brain still hadn't accepted the fact that Roxanne was serious. She was indeed leaving. And she expected Rachel to break the news to their father...and to David.

"Please don't be angry with me," Roxanne said, tears once more shining in her eyes. She put her arms around Rachel and hugged her hard. "I just can't help it. Tell David I'm sorry. I'm really sorry. But he'll be better off without me, you know he will."

Stunned, all Rachel could do was nod her agreement.

"I wish I could get my clothes, but they're all packed in the limousine." She started to leave, then stopped and pulled off her engagement ring—the ring Rachel loved so much—and handed it to Rachel. "I'll call you when I get to Mexico."

She gave Rachel another quick hug and kiss, and then she was gone, and Rachel was left standing there alone.

For a long moment she didn't move. She looked at the ring in her hand. It sparkled brilliantly under the fluorescent lighting. Then, slowly, she looked around. The beautiful lace wedding dress still hung in its plastic covering. The frothy veil still lay in its protective box. The white satin shoes with their pearls and little rosettes lay abandoned where Roxanne had left them, as abandoned as Rachel felt.

What was she going to do?

How was she going to go out there and face everyone?

She closed her eyes, imagined the disbelief and horror her news would generate.

Her mind whirled as the ramifications settled in. The church would soon be filled to capacity with hundreds of wedding guests. She could see her father and David, who were probably already out there, dressed in their tuxes, roses in their buttonholes...waiting.

She could imagine the eagerness in David's eyes, the happiness and anticipation he felt. She swallowed. Her stomach felt hollow. Dear God. He would be so humiliated and hurt in front of all of his family and friends. How could she possibly go out there and tell him? What could she possibly say to make things right?

And her father. She closed her eyes, shuddering as she thought about her father and what his reaction to this shocking news would be. He would be enraged. He would probably blame her. Didn't people always blame the messenger for bad tidings?

For a moment anger engulfed her, and she clenched her fists. How could Roxanne do this? Why hadn't she told David the truth, weeks ago, as Rachel had urged her to?

Oh, David, David...

As quickly as her anger had formed, it faded, leaving only a desperate wish that she could do something, *anything,* to keep from hurting him.

She loved him so much. Roxanne's desertion would be devastating, all the more so because it would be so public.

Rachel looked at the wall clock.

Twelve-fifty.

The church was probably already full. If only there was more time. If only all those people weren't already out there. If only she could tell him gently, in private, and they could concoct a face-saving story. At least then he could lick his wounds out of sight of all those curious—and pitying—eyes.

I can't do it. I can't go out there and tell him.

Once again her gaze moved to the beautiful wedding dress hanging a few feet away. How different things would be if she were the one engaged to David, if she were the one getting ready to go out there and marry him instead of Roxanne.

It should be me.

Suddenly, in the mirror across the room, she caught sight of herself standing there in her bridesmaid's dress that was still unzipped. And just as suddenly, she knew what she must do.

Heart pounding, she slipped Roxanne's engagement ring on her finger. Then, before she could change her mind, she stepped out of her dress and tossed it on a nearby chair. Next she kicked off her aquamarine pumps and put on Roxanne's white ones. She had to stuff facial tissue in the toes before they fit comfortably, because that was one of the few, minor differences between her and Roxanne. Roxanne's feet were half a size larger.

Once Rachel was satisfied with the feel of the shoes, she walked over to where the wedding dress hung. Her hands shook as she reached up and removed it from the hook. But somehow she managed to remove the plastic covering and put the dress on. She blessed the designer for putting a hidden zipper up the back instead of the tiny buttons that were so popular, because she knew she would never have been able to manage the buttons. The zipper was hard enough, but somehow she got the dress zipped up.

Calmer now, she lifted the veil out of the box and, walking to the mirror, placed it on her head, securing it with bobby pins. Once again, she blessed fate—and the hairdresser—for giving her the same hairstyle Roxanne had been wearing.

The veil settled into place.

A tremor snaked through Rachel as she looked at her image in the mirror. Large, frightened eyes stared back at her. For a few seconds she almost lost her nerve. What did she think she was doing? Was she crazy?

Maybe she was, but the alternative didn't bear thinking about. She could not go out there and tell David that Roxanne had deserted him.

Quickly, before Rachel could change her mind, she walked to the door that led to the vestibule and the waiting attendants. With her hand on the doorknob, Rachel whispered a hurried prayer. Then she took a deep breath, opened the door and walked out.

Chapter Four

Just as she'd pictured them, the wedding coordinator, the other four attendants and her father all waited in the vestibule. Paula Donofrio, Roxanne's best friend, was the first to spot Rachel. Her dark eyes lit up and, smiling, she rushed forward.

"Oh, Roxanne, you look so *gorgeous!*"

Soon everyone was milling around, exclaiming, oohing and aahing. Her father, looking handsome and proud, his blue eyes bright, stood to one side, beaming. When the attendants had finally stopped gushing, he walked slowly forward and reached for Rachel's hands.

"Angel. You look beautiful," he murmured. He gave her a tender smile and leaned forward to kiss her cheek. He smelled of his favorite aftershave and cologne.

Love and fear and the pain she always felt knowing her father loved Roxanne best churned inside her. "Thanks, Daddy," she whispered.

Liz Preston, the wedding coordinator, handed Rachel the bridal bouquet—an exquisite creation of orange blossoms, baby orchids and stephanotis. As Rachel took it, the flowers' fragrance drifted around her. Liz bustled about, straightening her veil, adjusting her train, as Rachel fought the tumult inside her. She wondered when someone would ask about her.

Finally Paula, looking around curiously, said, "Where's Rachel?"

This was the moment Rachel had been dreading, even though she knew exactly what she was going to say. She looked at her father. "I don't know how to tell you this, Daddy, but...Rachel is gone."

Her father frowned. "Gone? Gone where?"

"She...she left with a man she met several weeks ago. A man she's in love with."

For a moment, no one said a word. Then, as if at a director's cue, the attendants gasped and her father boomed, "What? You can't be serious! Rachel? Run off with some man? Where? And who in tarnation is he and why am I just now hearin' about him?"

Paula's eyes looked as if they were going to pop out as they met Rachel's gaze. Rachel shrugged the way she imagined Roxanne would have done if she had been the one standing here now. And then she began to tell the story of Carlos and Roxanne, substituting her own name in place of her sister's. It was amazing, but throughout the recitation Rachel's voice hardly quavered. In fact, as she talked, she became more and more sure that, under the circumstances, what she was doing was the only thing she *could* do.

It was also amazing that she could so easily deceive everyone, especially her father. Maybe it's true, she thought, that perception was everything. She had appeared in Roxanne's wedding dress, with Roxanne's engagement ring on her finger, and so, in the minds of everyone, she really *was* Roxanne. Knowing this gave her even more confidence.

"You mean to say that Rachel intends to *marry* this Carlos?" Sharon Lester, a childhood friend of both twins, asked. She was shaking her head in disbelief. "And she just took off, with no warning at all?"

"Yep," Rachel said, grinning the way Roxanne would have grinned. "I think it's kind of romantic, don't you?"

"I think it's unbelievable," Paula said. "I mean, this is your wedding day. How could she just go off like that? I don't understand why she couldn't at least wait until after the ceremony."

The others chimed in with their opinions, but just then, the strains of the wedding march sounded, and everyone fell silent.

Rachel looked at her father. This was the moment of truth. What would he do?

"None of this is important right now, sugar," he

finally said. "What's important here is you. This is your wedding day. Let's not let anything spoil it." He held out his right arm, and—trying hard to bury the pain his words had caused—she took it.

As Liz Preston lined everyone up and the first attendant began the hesitation step down the aisle, Rachel's father leaned closer. "I mean it now," he said, his voice hard. "You forget all about that sister of yours. I'll deal with her later."

Everything about the wedding was exactly the way Rachel had imagined it in her fantasies. The sun shining through the stained glass windows, gilding the assembled guests in shades of ruby, emerald and sapphire. The organ music, swelling in joyful crescendo as it heralded the approach of the bride. The scent of roses and camellias floating in the air. The tiny nosegays of flowers with streaming white ribbons that decorated the ends of each pew. The whispery rustle of silks and linens as the wedding guests turned to catch a glimpse of Rachel and her father making their slow way down the aisle. The solid feel of her father's arm guiding her slowly down the wide center aisle to the foot of the altar where David, backed by his groomsmen, waited.

David…

Rachel's heart skidded as her veiled gaze met his. *Oh, David.* She could hardly breathe. He looked so handsome. So wonderfully, incredibly handsome. And his smile! It lit up his face and caused a powerful rush of love to weaken her knees and constrict her chest.

As he'd been instructed at the rehearsal, her father stopped a few feet in front of the altar. Tearing her gaze away from David, Rachel turned to look up at her father. He smiled, his blue eyes filled with love and pride. For a moment, guilt flooded her as the reality of how she was deceiving these people she loved really hit her.

Don't think about it. You're committed now, so put it out of your mind. Just concentrate on getting through the day without giving yourself away.

As these thoughts swirled in her mind, Reverend Fitch, in the melodious voice Rachel had heard every Sunday since she was a little girl, began to speak.

"Dearly beloved, we are gathered here today in our beautiful church, in the sight of God and loving friends and family, to witness the marriage and commitment to each other of these two fine young people...." He gave them one of his beatific smiles. "I've known David Ross Hanson and Roxanne Alicia Carlton since they were children."

Hearing Roxanne's name spoken aloud was nearly Rachel's undoing. The words ricocheted in her mind.

Roxanne Alicia Carlton.

Everyone in this room believed she was her sister. But she, Rachel, was a liar and an impostor.

Dear heaven.

The magnitude of her deception made her head spin,

and her heart beat so fast and so hard she was certain everyone could hear it.

"And who gives Roxanne to be married to David?" continued the unsuspecting Reverend Fitch.

"I do," Rachel's father said. He released her hand and, taking it, placed it in David's.

As David's warm hand closed around hers, Rachel trembled. He squeezed her hand reassuringly, his eyes soft and loving, his smile for her alone.

Oh, David, darling David...my love...

Suddenly, as their gazes clung, all the guilt, all the fear and all the nervousness disappeared. A great calmness filled Rachel as together, her hand firmly and securely held in David's strong grasp, the two of them faced Reverend Fitch.

She had done the right thing, the only thing she could do, under the circumstances. Roxanne had really left her no choice. She knew that later that night she would have to tell David the truth. She also knew there would be consequences to face, but for now, she wouldn't think about any of that. For now, she would pretend she really was David's bride, and she would be happy for as long as the fantasy lasted.

The rest of the ceremony was dreamlike. Rachel made her responses and did everything she was supposed to do without hesitation. And then David slipped the wedding ring—a narrow circle of diamonds—onto her finger, where it joined Roxanne's engagement ring, and the minister said, "I now pronounce you husband and wife."

At his words, Paula, who had stepped in as maid of honor now that the supposed maid of honor had disappeared, lifted the veil away from Rachel's face. Then David put his arms around her, and his lips met hers in a kiss so sweet and so loving, it touched Rachel to her very soul. Slowly they drew apart, and he smiled down at her.

In that moment Rachel would have given anything on earth to really be Mrs. David Hanson—not just today, but for the rest of her life.

Triumphant organ music resounded through the church, and David, grinning widely, clasped her hand and the two of them walked quickly down the aisle amidst a sea of smiling guests.

Reaching the vestibule, Rachel and David, along with their attendants, Rachel's father, and David's grandmother, formed the official receiving line. Rachel's dreamlike state continued as she received the kisses and hugs and congratulatory handshakes. She found it was easy to smile and thank people for coming and she even managed to answer questions about the absent "Rachel" without any slipups.

Her only close call came when Kurt Avery, a fellow teacher and someone she had dated a few times the previous month, came up to her. Unthinkingly, she smiled and greeted him by name.

He gave her a puzzled smile. "How'd you know who I was?"

Immediately she realized her mistake. Roxanne had never met Kurt.

"Oh, Rachel pointed you out to me one day," she said, hardly missing a beat. "She told me what a nice guy you are." She smiled in the flirty way Roxanne always smiled at men. "And she didn't exaggerate."

He chuckled, but his eyes were speculative as they studied hers. "Obviously not that nice, since she's run off with another man."

Rachel laughed, too, but inside she was quaking. She would have to be more careful or she would be unmasked before she ever left the church.

Rachel drew a deep breath of relief when he moved away. After that, there were only a few more guests to be greeted before it was time to leave for the reception. As they walked outside to the waiting cars, Hank fell into step with her and David.

"Did Rachel really run off to Mexico to marry a guy none of you have ever met?" he asked.

Rachel nodded.

"Hank had designs on Rachel, himself," David said, his eyes twinkling.

Rachel hoped the surprise she felt didn't show in her face. She'd had no idea Hank was interested in her. "I'm sorry."

"Hey, nothing for you to feel sorry about," he said. "That's the breaks."

By now, most of the wedding party had piled into the waiting cars for the short drive to the country club. Hank and Rachel had been scheduled to ride with David and Roxanne, and Rachel felt sorry for Hank, who seemed to feel awkward now. "You can still ride with us," she offered.

"No." He shook his head. "That's okay. I'll ride with Steve."

"Okay, see you there," David said, putting his arm around Rachel's waist and guiding her to the limousine parked at the end of the front walkway. The driver smiled and held the back door open.

Once inside the plush car, David drew her close, tipping her chin up so he could look into her eyes. "I can't believe we're finally married," he said softly.

"I can't either," Rachel said. Her heart was beating too fast.

He bent down, his mouth capturing hers in a long, thrilling kiss that left Rachel breathless.

"I'm also glad Hank didn't come along for the ride," he said when he finally broke the kiss.

"Me, too."

The teasing twinkle in David's eyes faded as he studied her upturned face. "I love you, Mrs. Hanson," he murmured.

"I love you, too," she said fervently. "I've loved you all of my life." It felt wonderful to say aloud the words she'd thought so many times, the words she'd never believed she would ever be able to say.

"Really? All of your life?"

"All of my life," she whispered. "There's never been anyone else."

He held her close again. "We're going to be so happy, Roxanne."

Roxanne.

Rachel swallowed, blinking back tears. If only she could stop time. If only she really *were* Roxanne.

"Hey, why the tears?" he said, even though she tried to unobtrusively wipe them away. "I thought you were happy."

"I *am* happy. I—I always cry when I'm happy."

"You do?"

She nodded.

"There are a lot of things I don't know about you, aren't there?" he said after a moment.

Rachel once again felt miserable. David was such a nice man. And this was such a not-nice thing she and Roxanne had done to him.

"Aw, sweetheart, come on," he coaxed. "If you're so happy, let's see you smile."

Rachel did her best, and thankfully, just then, the limo driver pulled in to the curved driveway of the country club, and in the flurry and excitement of arrival, Rachel's spirits lifted.

Hand in hand, they walked into the large ballroom where most of the guests were already gathered, and Rachel steeled herself for another round of questions and incredulity over "Rachel's" defection.

"This is just so hard to believe," said Melissa Chasan, a mutual friend of the twins, who, along with her husband, Joel, had been exclaiming over Rachel's uncharacteristic behavior for the past fifteen minutes. "I mean, Rachel's always been so *predictable.* She's never done anything spontaneous in her life!"

"I know," David said. "Running off on the spur of the moment is more like something *you'd* do." He squeezed Rachel's waist.

"Did you have any idea she was thinking of eloping with this Carlos?" Melissa pressed, looking at Rachel.

"No," Rachel said, trying to tell as much of the truth as possible, although she had decided not to disclose that Carlos had actually come to the church. "I mean, I knew she had met him and that she had fallen in love with him, *really* in love with him...and, well, I also knew he'd asked her to marry him, but I thought she'd decided against it." She kept her gaze away from David as she spoke. He was so honest, it was hard to look into his eyes when she was being anything but. "I guess, in the end, she just couldn't bear the thought of him leaving without her."

Another guest—a pretty blond woman who looked to be in her early forties—obviously overheard the conversation, for she moved closer and, sighing, said, "It's so terribly romantic, what your sister did." She held out her hand. "Lisa Gavin. I'm Blaine Gavin's wife."

"Oh," Rachel said, although she had no idea who Blaine Gavin was. "It's nice to meet you."

"And you, too. Blaine has talked about you ever since you did your first seminar for the company."

Oh, great, Rachel thought, *a customer of Roxanne's and definitely someone she would be expected to know.* "Um, is Blaine here? I haven't seen him." She didn't remember seeing Lisa Gavin at the church, so she felt safe saying this.

Lisa smiled. "Yes, he's here. He's gone to the bar to get us a drink. I'm sorry we weren't able to make it to the church."

This masquerade was going to be harder to pull off than Rachel had thought. *Thought? You didn't think! You just acted. If you'd* really *thought about this, you'd never have done it.* But she *had* done it, so she'd better concentrate on doing it right, hadn't she?

For the next hour it seemed to Rachel that all she did was answer incredulous questions. The guests were abuzz about what her twin had done. Wryly, she wondered what they'd say if they knew the truth. They'd be more than abuzz. They'd be stunned.

One of these days they will *know the truth.* Oh, wouldn't the gossip mavens have a field day when the real story was out.

Resolutely, she pushed the depressing thoughts away. She couldn't afford to indulge her guilty feelings. Not now. She still had hours to go before she would have that luxury.

All the talk and speculation about Rachel succeeded in getting her father stirred up again. He gave voice to his feelings when he claimed Rachel for a dance.

"I'm sorry, sugar," he said as he led her expertly through a foxtrot.

"Sorry for what, Daddy?"

"Sorry that your sister has succeeded in ruining your day."

"It's okay, really. I'm not...mad at Rachel. I understand."

"I'm glad you do, because I sure as hell don't. Why couldn't she tell me about this man instead of sneaking off like a coward? And why did she have to pick today to do it?"

"Maybe she—"

"Maybe nothing! There's no excuse for what she did, and let me tell you, little girl, your sister is going to be sorry. And that...that *man*, whoever the hell he is, is going to be even sorrier. Nobody messes with Wylie Carlton and gets away with it. He probably thinks he's got a one-way ticket to my money. Well, believe you me, he couldn't be more wrong."

"I don't think he wants your money, Daddy," Rachel said stiffly. She was trying hard not to feel hurt by her father's assessment of her character—not that it came as any real surprise. Hadn't he insinuated she was spineless many times? "Just like her mother, God rest her soul," he was wont to say, shaking his head sadly. "Afraid of her own shadow."

Rachel wondered if he'd take this position if he knew which one of his daughters had *really* run off to marry Carlos Terraza. She had no doubt her father would still be hurt and upset, but she also felt he'd get over his upset pretty quickly once Roxanne cried prettily and said how much she loved him and begged him to forgive her.

"Damn good thing for him if he doesn't," her father continued, his eyes hard, "because he'll never see a penny of it. I'm goin' over to Mark Ingram's office first thing Monday morning and cut Rachel right out of my will."

Rachel fought not to give way to the emotions churning inside her. She wanted to say if it had really been her who'd run off to marry the man she loved, she wouldn't care if her father *did* cut her out of his will, because she'd never cared anything about his money. She wanted to say that all she'd ever wanted from Wylie was the same love and understanding and admiration he gave so freely to Roxanne. She wanted to say that he'd never given her a chance and now, when she needed his support and understanding the most, he refused to even try to understand. Of course, she could say none of these things. She wasn't Rachel right now, she was Roxanne, the fair-haired daughter. If she gave voice to her thoughts, she would be bound to give herself away.

And let's face it, she told herself bitterly, *now, after what you've pulled today, you would deserve everything he's thought about you all these years, anyway, wouldn't you? In fact, he'd have every right to despise you.*

She was caught in a trap of her own making. For the first time in her life she was ready to defend herself, and couldn't.

For the rest of their dance she was miserable and could barely manage to paste a smile on her face. But finally the dance was over and she could escape her father's anger and disappointment.

During the remainder of the reception, Rachel danced and ate and talked to the guests and pretended to be happy, but all the happiness she'd felt during the ceremony had faded and now her only emotions were a deepening melancholy and hopelessness as the hour when she would have to face David with the truth came closer and closer.

Roxanne was tired, David thought, watching her from a distance. Obviously, the stress of Rachel's defection on top of the normal stress of the wedding had been too much. He looked at his watch—4:45. Thank God. Only fifteen more minutes and they could leave.

He smiled, thinking of their upcoming honeymoon trip. He had rented a private villa in Colombé—one he'd seen a few years earlier when he and two of his buddies had spent a week on the island. The villa was rented out by its discriminating owner to only a few, select people. It was perfect, David thought, situated on a small rise overlooking a cove about a hundred feet from the sheltered beach. It had a beautiful view, and as far as he had been able to tell, almost complete privacy.

He couldn't wait to show the villa to Roxanne. He couldn't wait to get her there, alone, where they could rest and eat and swim and sun themselves...and make love.

His body stirred at the thought.

His wife.

From this day forward.

His wife.

"I'll help you get changed," Paula said.

"Thanks," said Rachel.

"But first you have to throw the bouquet."

"Oh, I forgot about that."

"I know." Paula smiled. "That's okay. I didn't."

Paula, dragging Rachel with her, walked up to the stage and announced that all single women present should come forward. Within minutes, about fifty laughing, chattering women congregated at the foot of the stage below where Rachel stood. Laughing, she turned her back to them and tossed the bouquet over her shoulder.

A squealing girl of about eighteen, whose name Rachel didn't remember, caught it. "Ooh," she said, "I'm next!"

Finally Rachel and Paula were free to head upstairs to the private dressing room where Roxanne's going-away clothes waited. Paula unlocked the door and the two women went inside.

After helping Rachel remove the wedding dress and veil, Paula reached for the peach silk slacks and matching jacket Roxanne had chosen and brought over yesterday. "I *love* this outfit."

"Yes," Rachel said, "me, too." The slacks, shell top and jacket fit almost perfectly, and if the waistband of the slacks were a bit looser than they would have been on Roxanne, Rachel didn't think anyone would notice.

Once she was dressed, she took her hair down and brushed it out, letting it fall in its natural curly state to her shoulders. Looking at herself in the mirror, she wished she could erase the signs of strain in her eyes, but she was afraid they would remain there until she had unburdened herself to David. Knowing that soon she would have to tell him the truth felt like a ten-ton weight on her shoulders.

She reached for Roxanne's soft brown leather shoulder bag, which had also been placed in the room earlier. Turning to Paula, she said brightly, "Guess I'm ready."

"One more thing," Paula said, reaching for the small corsage that had been cleverly integrated into the bridal bouquet. She smiled and pinned the flowers to Rachel's shoulder. "There," she said, standing back. "You look perfect."

Without warning, Rachel's eyes filled with tears.

Paula's face melted into concern. "Hey, what's wrong?"

"N-nothing," Rachel said hastily. "I—I guess I'm just nervous."

"Don't be." Paula smiled reassuringly. "David's a good guy. He'll make a great husband." She put her arms around Rachel and hugged her. "I know you've had some doubts, but heck, everyone does. I almost bolted on my wedding day, but after it was all over and Craig and I were on our honeymoon, everything was fine, and I was really glad I'd married him."

Rachel didn't trust herself to speak. Instead, she returned Paula's hug and nodded. Then, together, they headed downstairs.

David, his grandmother, Rachel's father, the rest of the wedding party and as many guests as could fit into the entrance hall of the club all waited at the foot of the curving staircase. David had changed from his black tux into sharply creased tan designer slacks and an open-necked pale yellow shirt worn with a light-weight darker brown sport coat. He looked wonderful, Rachel thought, but then, he always looked wonderful to her.

He smiled up at her, his admiring eyes telling her how much he loved her.

How much he loves Roxanne, not you.

Rachel forced a smile to her lips.

Then it was another round of teasing and well-wishing to be endured. Georgina Hanson waited until the guests and wedding attendants had had their turn, then she came up to Rachel. Her shining dark eyes, so like David's, were filled with affection. "You and David have made me very happy, my dear," she said softly as they hugged. "To have our families united, well, it's the fulfillment of a lifelong wish."

"I'm glad," Rachel said. She wondered if, after finding out the truth, David's grandmother would ever speak to her again. It hurt terribly to think that Georgina might not.

Last to say goodbye before David and Rachel left was Rachel's father. He enveloped her in a bear hug. "Love you, angel," he said gruffly.

"I love you, too, Daddy."

His eyes were suspiciously bright as he released her. He turned to David and shook his hand. "You take good care of her, son."

"Oh, I will, Mr. Carlton."

Two minutes later, amid a shower of rice, David and Rachel were running down the shallow front steps toward the waiting limousine.

Rachel's heart was heavy, and to smile and laugh and pretend to be happy was one of the hardest things she'd ever had to do. One thought kept going around and around in her head. In just minutes she would have to tell David the truth. *Please God,* she prayed as David helped her into the sleek car, *give me the strength to do this wisely and well.*

She continued to silently pray as David, surrounded by his groomsmen, attempted to break away and join her inside.

The groomsmen were having none of it. Before David could protest or keep them out, all three of them climbed into the limo with Rachel. Steve O'Hara, who had been a high school classmate of David's, laughed at Rachel's surprised expression. "We're going to the airport with you," he said. "Give you a proper send-off."

Soon Paula joined them. Her expression was apologetic. "This wasn't my idea, but Craig and I agreed that as long as these bozos were determined to come with you, I'd better come, too. Give you some moral support."

A resigned David finally climbed in next to Rachel. He put his arm around her. "Sorry about this," he said.

"It...it's okay."

But it wasn't okay, because how was Rachel going to tell him the truth now? She couldn't. Not here. Not in front of his friends.

She sank back against the seat in weary resignation.

There was no help for it.

She would have to continue her charade a while longer.

Chapter Five

The drive to the airport was a nightmare.

Just when she'd thought she could finally be herself, Rachel had to work even harder at being Roxanne.

It was excruciating.

She had to smile. And laugh. And endure the teasing and sexual innuendo that became more bawdy the closer they got to Intercontinental.

Several times she came close to losing it, but somehow she hung on. The trip would be over soon. The limo driver had just entered the ramp from Beltway 8 to John F. Kennedy Boulevard, which led directly into the airport.

Just hold on for another ten minutes, and then they'll be gone.

"So where are you guys staying in Miami?" Steve asked.

"Oh, no," David replied, grinning. His arm around Rachel tightened protectively. "That's our secret."

"Aw, come on," said Jason Turnbull, another of the groomsmen who'd come along for the ride. "You can tell us. It isn't like we're going to follow you down there."

"Forget it," David said.

"Why are you going to Miami, anyway?" Hank asked. "Why not just go straight to Colombé?"

"Because there were no flights to the islands tonight," David said. "And I knew better than to stay in Houston."

Hank poked Jason in the ribs. "Smart man."

Jason grinned. "Yeah, we'd have been sure to find you if you had."

"Exactly," David said.

"Remember how we found Rob and Judy?" Steve said.

Jason chortled.

Because Hank didn't know what they were talking about, Steve and Jason explained the way they'd tormented another friend and his bride on their wedding night.

"You guys are juvenile, you know that?" Paula said.

"Aw, it's all in fun," Steve said. "We only bugged 'em for about an hour, then we left 'em alone."

They continued to tease and joke, and by the time

the limo pulled up in front of Terminal C, Rachel was completely exhausted. The strain of pretending the presence of the others was funny, which was exactly what Roxanne would have thought, had taken its toll, and she couldn't wait to get away from them.

The limo driver parked at the curb, and the guys helped David remove their luggage from the trunk. Then, while David's back was turned, Steve slipped the limo driver some money, and the limo took off toward the parking garage.

Rachel was dismayed.

Paula grimaced. "I guess we're goin' inside with you guys."

David just shook his head when he realized there would be no getting away from the exuberant groomsmen until he and Rachel were actually on the plane.

The Continental curbside agent checked their tickets and ID, and once their luggage was on the conveyor belt, Rachel and David—surrounded by their laughing attendants—headed for the security checkpoint.

Rachel desperately wished Houston's airport prohibited all but actual passengers from going to the gate, but unfortunately, anyone who passed the security check was allowed to enter. There would be no getting away from Hank, Steve, Jason and Paula.

What was she going to do? She certainly couldn't talk to David while they were with them.

And the unwanted attendants were creating such a scene! Dressed as they were in their wedding finery, and with all their hoots and jokes and laughter, they were making it impossible for anyone to mistake David and Rachel for anything other than newlyweds. Rachel wouldn't have minded if she was really a bride, but she wasn't. She was a fake, and she was exhausted, and she just wanted Steve and Jason and Hank and Paula to go home and leave them alone.

The wait for their boarding call seemed interminable. It was all Rachel could do to keep a smile on her face. Several times David gave her a sympathetic look. "It won't be long now," he murmured, putting his arm around her.

If he only knew her inner turmoil. Of course, if he knew what was bothering her, she wouldn't *be* in such turmoil. Rachel couldn't believe this was happening. It was as if all the mischievous forces in the universe were at work and conspiring to keep her from telling David the truth.

What was she going she do? she asked herself again.

You'll have to get on the plane. There's nothing else you can *do.*

Just then, one of the gate attendants picked up a hand mike and announced that Flight 1811 to Miami would now begin boarding. David and Rachel stood. They held first-class tickets, so they would be among the first to board.

"Okay, you guys, this is it. We're leaving," David said good-naturedly.

Hank clapped him on the back. "Enjoy, old buddy."

Paula gave Rachel another hug, and each of the guys kissed her cheek. When it was Hank's turn, he said, "I hope you're not mad at us."

"No," she said.

Hank smiled. "David's a lucky guy."

Oh, God, she thought, *if you only knew...*

"I'm sorry, sweetheart," David said when they finally escaped the groomsmen. "If I could've figured out a way to get rid of them, I would have."

"I know. It's okay." For one wild moment she considered telling David the truth right then, in the jetway, because otherwise she would have to board the plane. But she immediately realized how untenable the idea was. There was no way she could do that to David.

You have to get on the plane.

Five minutes later she and David were settled into their seats in the second row. "Alone, finally," he said. He took her hand.

Rachel looked at their linked fingers. Her rings sparkled under the overhead lights.

Roxanne's rings, not yours. Just then, Rachel looked up. Her eyes met those of an attractive older woman seated next to an equally attractive older man who sat across the aisle from them.

"Congratulations," the woman said. "I'm assuming, from the little going-away party you had back there, that you two are newlyweds."

Even though Rachel felt totally miserable, she couldn't help smiling back, because the woman had such a sweet smile and such nice, friendly eyes.

"We just got married this afternoon." David's voice rang with pride.

The woman turned to her husband. "John and I will be married forty-eight years next month."

"Forty-eight *happy* years," her husband said gallantly. His hazel-eyed gaze turned to David. "And I hope you'll be just as happy with your beautiful wife as I've been with my Margaret."

David's hand tightened around Rachel's. "I'm sure I will be."

Rachel's smile faltered around the lump in her throat.

"Just remember," the woman said, "to love each other well and never go to bed mad."

"That's right," her husband agreed. Then he laughed. "Although, if you *do* go to bed mad, making up can be a lot of fun, too."

"Oh, John," the woman said, ducking her head in embarrassment.

David chuckled and squeezed Rachel's hand again.

The woman and her husband soon began to carry on a private conversation, and David, leaning closer, lifted her hand and kissed it. "Some day we'll be like them."

Oh, David, if only that were true...

"I can't wait until tonight," he continued, his voice lower now and more intimate. "I've been thinking about it for so long." He nuzzled her ear, his breath warm. "I want you so much."

Rachel could hardly breathe.

For a long moment they looked into each other's eyes. She moistened her lips, and his gaze followed.

He's going to kiss me.

She could see the desire in his eyes. A second later his head dipped, and his mouth sought hers.

The kiss was thrilling—filled with promise and passion—and it caused Rachel to forget everything and everyone except David and how much she loved him and wanted him, too.

You could have him. All you'd have to do is continue to keep quiet.

Everything in her went still at the thought.

Keep quiet.

If she didn't tell David the truth, if she went on pretending to be Roxanne...

No!

She couldn't do that. She couldn't. It was too awful.

Why can't you? You've gone this far. Why not go all the way? For once, do what Roxanne would do. Take what you want.

Rachel remembered the passionate expression on Roxanne's face when she had said she was seizing her chance at happiness.

All her life Rachel had been timid. She had never seized anything.

This was her chance. The only one she might ever have.

Yes, there would be consequences.

Yes, when David found out the truth, she would have to pay those consequences.

But she would have to, anyway, whether she told David the truth now or told him later.

Rachel loved David with all her heart, and she wanted this time with him. Maybe she couldn't have him for a lifetime, but she *could* have him for a week.

One glorious week...

Rachel's heart pounded at the thought.

A week. One whole week, alone, with David.

If she never had anything else in her life, she would at least have memories.

But what about the September show? What about all the work you have to do? If you go to Colombé, you'll lose seven painting days. Can you afford to do that?

She would have the rest of her life to paint. This opportunity to be with David would never come again.

Surely she could make up the lost painting time over the remainder of the summer. She would just work harder, that's all.

She looked at David. At his strong profile. At the tiny bump on the bridge of his nose. At the endearing cowlick on the crown of his head. At his mouth. That wonderful mouth.

She remembered the way he'd kissed her last week, on the night he'd mistaken her for Roxanne. She remembered the feel of his hands on her body. Even now, the memory caused warmth to spread through her.

She leaned her head back. Closed her eyes.

Do it! For once in your life, take what you want.

In that moment her decision was made. For the next week she would continue to be Roxanne, and damn the consequences.

David had booked a suite at the Fontainebleau. It was Rachel's first visit to Miami, and even though she was nervous about the coming night, and still tired from the stress of the day, she was delighted when the taxi pulled up in front of the famed hotel. Her pleasure intensified when, fifteen minutes later, they were shown into their beautiful suite with its ocean view.

"Oh, David, it's wonderful," she said.

He beamed.

After dealing with their luggage, the bellman walked around and pointed out items of special interest, then opened the sliding glass door that led to their private balcony. Fresh sea breezes filled the room, as well as the muted sounds of Collins Avenue and Miami Beach nightlife far below.

"Will there be anything else, sir?" the bellman said with an expectant smile.

"I think that's everything," David said, tipping him generously.

The bellman left, and finally the two of them were alone.

For a few seconds they stood there awkwardly, neither quite knowing what to do. Rachel's pleasure began to fade as doubts crept in. She told herself not to be nervous, but she couldn't help it. It was one thing to say she was going to seize her chance. It was quite another to actually do it.

What if she couldn't pull this off?

What if, the moment David began to make love to her, he realized she was an impostor?

Rachel knew Roxanne and David had not been intimate yet, because Roxanne had confessed as much one day. Even so, they had been seeing one another for more than a year. Perhaps they hadn't completed the act of love, but they had certainly shared intimate kisses and caresses.

What if he *knew?*

He didn't know when he was kissing you earlier.

True, but a few kisses and the act of making love were two very different things, she reminded herself. Two *very* different things.

"Is something wrong with the room?" David asked.

"No, of course not," she said hurriedly. "I, um, guess I should unpack my overnight bag." She couldn't meet David's eyes.

Stop acting like an idiot! Now you've got him worried.

But no matter how sternly she berated herself, her stomach continued to feel as if someone had tied it in knots. Avoiding his gaze, she opened the overnight bag. At least she'd seen all of Roxanne's trousseau, so there was no hesitation. Unerringly, she reached for the nightgown Roxanne had chosen—a slinky concoction of pale blue lace and satin.

David touched her arm. "Sweetheart..."

Rachel jumped, now completely flustered.

"Listen, after you get unpacked, why don't you take a nice, long, relaxing bath?" he suggested.

Rachel could have hugged him. Dear David. He was so thoughtful. He knew she was nervous, and he was telling her it was okay, that he understood, that he wouldn't rush her. Giving him a grateful smile, she said, "That's a great idea. I think I will."

Ten minutes later Rachel escaped into the privacy of the large, luxurious bathroom with its oversize tub. She turned the hot water jets on full force and poured in strawberry-scented bath oil. When her bath was ready, she slowly lowered herself into the fragrant water. Closing her eyes, she willed her body to relax.

She tried not to think about the sexy nightgown and how it would reveal much more than it concealed. She tried not to think about how she knew nothing of what might please David and what might not. She tried not to think about all the ways in which she could fail. She tried only to concentrate on how much she loved David and how much she wanted him.

Because if she didn't, she just might lose her nerve.

Once Rachel disappeared into the bathroom, David raided the minibar. He fixed himself a glass of brandy, then changed into black silk pajama bottoms. After turning off the lights—leaving the bedroom lit only by moonlight—he carried his drink outside to the balcony. Barefoot, he stood at the rail and listened to the surf and the muted sounds of Miami nightlife far below.

The night air felt cool on his skin, although he imagined the temperature was still somewhere in the eighties. The full moon shone brightly in the star-studded, navy night. He could hear seagulls squawking and horns tooting and lilting salsa music coming from the suite next door. Lights from boats winked in the distance.

He sipped his drink and listened and looked out to sea and thought about how, so many times, he'd questioned his choices in life. Even this one had caused him some doubt. But no longer. From the moment he'd set eyes on Roxanne walking down the aisle of St. John's earlier in the day, all his misgivings had disappeared. She was meant to be his wife, and very soon she would be his wife in every sense of the word.

He smiled. She was nervous. He couldn't remember the last time he'd seen Roxanne nervous about anything. She had always been so bold and so unafraid, and those traits were part of what he loved about her.

Yet tonight, seeing that she, too, could be vulnerable, had endeared her to him in a way her strengths had not, and had brought out all his protective instincts.

He let himself think about the upcoming night, let the desire he'd tamped down for so long begin to build. Anticipation heated his blood and quickened his breathing. He was suddenly very glad they'd waited until now to make love, because it would be even more special than if they'd already become lovers.

He imagined the way she would look in the delicate gown she'd taken out of her suitcase, imagined the way her skin would feel when he touched her and kissed her, imagined the way he would feel when they finally consummated their love, and by the time he heard the bathroom door opening about twenty minutes later, his body thrummed with need.

He slowly turned.

Roxanne stood in the spill of light from the bathroom. Her slender body in the revealing blue nightgown took his breath away.

He put down his glass and, leaving the balcony door open, walked into the room. Her gaze slowly met his, and he saw that she was chewing on her lower lip. Tenderness flooded him as he realized she was still nervous, even though she was trying hard to pretend she wasn't.

Vowing he would be gentle, he took her hand and led her to the bed. Sitting beside her, he enfolded her in his arms.

Go slowly, he reminded himself as he lowered his mouth to hers. *Make this good for her.* He had to hold back a moan as her mouth opened under his and he tasted its sweetness and the erotic tangle of her tongue.

He hadn't forgotten his admonitions to be patient and tender, but his good intentions crumbled under the force of his need for her and the eager way she responded to him.

"Roxanne," he said gruffly, kissing her again and again. "Roxanne."

Tearing his mouth from hers, he buried his face in the inviting hollow between her small, firm breasts. His heart pounded and his body burned with a desire that threatened to rage out of control as he pushed the thin straps of her nightgown down around her shoulders. He lifted first one then the other breast to his mouth. He had fantasized about this so many times, but the reality was better than the fantasy. Her nipples peaked into hard nubs as he laved them, and now she was moaning and writhing under him.

The sound was nearly his undoing. It took all his willpower to keep from taking her then, but somehow he slowed down. Lifting his face, he took a long, unsteady breath and caressed her cheek.

"Let's get rid of these clothes," he said in a ragged voice that didn't sound like his at all.

"Yes," she agreed.

Rachel's fears and doubts had disappeared for good the moment he began to kiss her.

Yes, yes, she'd thought. *Yes. This is what I want.* Her body had bloomed under his touch, and soon she resented even the thin layer of clothing that separated them. She wanted to feel his skin next to hers. She wanted to touch him the way he was touching her. She wanted more than touches. She wanted him to kiss her everywhere. She wanted him to do the things to her she'd only imagined or read about. She wanted to feel him inside her, to know what it meant to give herself to the man she loved.

So when David suggested they undress, she was ready. In just moments, her nightgown and his pajama bottoms lay in a shining heap on the floor, and then David was doing all the things she'd wanted him to do.

She gloried in his touch, closing her eyes and giving herself up to the exquisite sensations as he explored her body. She reveled in them, gasping when his mouth replaced his hands, because the way he made her feel was such sweet torture and she never wanted him to stop.

"Do you like this?" he said, his fingers slipping inside her.

"Oh, yes, yes."

"Do you want me to stop?" He began to stroke her.

Heart nearly bursting, she could hardly answer as she strained against him. She was on fire with wanting him. She knew she wouldn't be able to hold back if he didn't stop, and yet she couldn't make herself say the words. "No," she finally gasped.

And then she was falling apart around him, in wave after wave of intense pleasure that threatened to shatter her.

He entered her in one swift thrust, and she was more than ready. She wrapped her arms and legs around him tightly and they began to move together to find their rhythm.

Nothing had prepared her for this moment and the truth of it. Holding David, feeling him deep inside her, Rachel's heart soared with the knowledge that in a world where too many things were wrong, this moment and this man and the love they were sharing were very, very right.

"I love you," she said.

"I love you," he gasped just before he gave one final thrust and exploded into her.

Afterward, as their bodies cooled and their hearts slowed and their breaths became even, she lay in the circle of David's arms and felt his warm breath against her cheek and the quiet pleasure of his hand idly caressing her breast and thought that no matter what happened in the future, she would never be sorry about this night.

And this was only the beginning!

She had an entire week to look forward to—a week where they would make love again and again. And maybe, if she was very lucky, she would take something more than just memories away from the week.

Maybe she would be pregnant.

Chapter Six

Now, where did *that* thought come from? she wondered. *Maybe it was always there. Maybe, from the minute you decided to seize this week with David, that was the idea all along.*

David's baby. Oh, if only she *could* get pregnant!

Her heart beat faster. A part of him to treasure always.

She lay very still and let the idea build.

If she *did* become pregnant, what would she do? She couldn't tell David. She would never want him to feel obligated to her or responsible for her, especially since, when he knew the truth, he would probably despise her.

You wouldn't have *to tell him.*

True. She could go away somewhere. After all, she could paint anywhere, and with her credentials at the academy, she could probably get a teaching job elsewhere, too. And even if she couldn't, she and her baby would never starve. After all, it wasn't as if she was destitute, or anything. Even if her father disowned her—and he might, once he found out what she'd done—she had her inheritance from her mother. Granted, it wasn't riches, but it was enough to buy a small house.

And she had her car and her furniture. And her half of the town house she and Roxanne jointly owned. If they sold it—and surely Roxanne would want to, now that she was living in Mexico—it would give Rachel a nest egg for the future.

She could manage just fine.

David's baby...

She fell asleep dreaming about the possibility.

She was so different from what he'd imagined she would be, David thought as he watched her sleep. Sweeter, softer, shyer. Yet this Roxanne, with her newly revealed vulnerability, suited him perfectly.

She looked younger asleep, all the brittleness and edginess that had been so pronounced in the past month completely erased from her face. Her chest rose and fell gently, and every once in a while she would sigh and there would be a faint smile on her face.

He brushed his lips across the delicate curve of her cheek, inhaling the faint fragrance that clung to her skin and marveling that this sexy, beautiful, desirable woman—a woman who could have had her choice of just about any man—had chosen him.

His wife.

Pride and love nearly overwhelmed him. She was his wife, and she was perfect. And making love to her had been perfect. He liked the fact that she'd been shy at first, but he liked it even better afterward, when she lost her shyness. She'd been everything he'd dreamed of, and more. Her passion had matched his, fueled his. There had been no holding back. She had shown him, in her every reaction, how much she wanted him.

He let his gaze trail to her barely covered breasts, to the inviting swell of her hip, the long length of her shapely leg, part of which was uncovered. Her feet were small and narrow, with high arches. Her toenails were painted a deep pink. Looking at them made him want her. Everything about her made him want her.

He could hardly believe she was his. That for the rest of their lives, they would be together.

He lifted a stray strand of her silky hair, smoothing it back and away from her face.

She sighed and stirred. David took advantage of the opportunity to gently slide his arm out from under her. Then he quietly got up. Taking care not to make noise, he put on his pajama bottoms and walked to the mini-bar, where he fixed himself another small glass of brandy. Then he sat in one of the two armchairs flanking the open balcony door and propped his feet on the bottom of the bed. He slowly sipped his brandy and listened to the surf and watched his wife sleep.

His wife.

He thought about the older couple they'd talked to on the flight to Miami. He and Roxanne would be exactly like that. In love no matter how long they were married.

He smiled, remembering what it had been like when he'd come back to Houston after spending three years in Saudi Arabia. It was the middle of November, a year and a half ago, and he'd been home for only a couple of days. He was staying at his grandmother's while looking for a place of his own, and she'd waylaid him before he left that morning, saying she'd invited the Carltons for dinner that night. "You *are* going to be here, aren't you?" she'd asked anxiously. "You don't have any other plans?"

David had smiled. "Sure. It'll be great seeing them all again."

"It'll just be Roxanne and Wylie," his grandmother said.

"Oh? Rachel can't come?"

"I thought you knew. Rachel's in France on sabbatical. She had an opportunity to study with Gaulier."

"No, I didn't know." David was disappointed that he wouldn't get to see both twins, but the moment Roxanne and her father walked into his grandmother's house, he completely forgot his disappointment. It was as if the years of separation between him and Roxanne had never existed. He immediately fell under her spell, just as he had when they were kids, and he'd been captivated ever since.

Over the next months he pursued her, continuing to ask her out, even though she kept refusing, saying she was involved with someone else. He finally wore her down, and she accepted a date for a movie and dinner. They'd had a great time together, laughing and talking. She fascinated him. Her energy and passion for life were exactly what he needed and wanted.

That had been the beginning. From then on, he had been relentless. He would not allow her to forget he was there.

It hadn't been easy. Roxanne wasn't one to be pinned down without a struggle. But eventually his patience and persistence—combined with a little help from her father—had paid off, and the following October she was wearing David's engagement ring on her finger and they'd set their wedding date for the next summer. David hadn't wanted to wait that long before getting married, but Roxanne had been adamant.

"There's no rush," she'd said. "It's only eight and a half months, and weddings take at least that much time to plan. Besides, I've always wanted to be a June bride."

It hadn't been easy to wait.

But the waiting was over now, he thought triumphantly. Roxanne was his. Draining his glass, he climbed into bed beside her. Careful not to awaken her, he put his arms around her and cradled her close. Filled with a deep contentment, he closed his eyes and allowed sleep to take him, too.

Rachel stretched lazily, slowly opening her eyes. A smiling David—hair wet and slicked back, tanned and muscular torso wrapped in one of the thick white towels furnished by the hotel, and looking wonderfully sexy and handsome—sat watching her from his perch at the side of the bed.

"Good morning, sleepyhead." He leaned over to kiss her cheek. "I thought you were going to sleep all morning."

Rachel smiled shyly. "Good morning." She stretched. "What time is it?"

"Nine o'clock."

"Umm." She stretched again. "What time does our plane leave?"

"Not until two. Don't worry. I was just teasing you. We have plenty of time." David moved closer and, reaching out, caressed her hip, his warm hand moving in slow, sensuous strokes. Delightful shivers raced down her spine. His hungry gaze fastened on hers as his hand slowly stole up to cup her breast. Rachel's pulse quickened, and her breathing became shallow as his thumb gently stroked back and forth.

He bent to kiss her, and she knew he wanted to make love. "Wait just a minute, okay?"

He grinned. "Okay."

She scrambled out of bed, grabbed her discarded

nightgown from the floor and, without looking in David's direction, hurried into the bathroom.

By the time she'd brushed her teeth and hair, washed her face, put her nightgown back on and returned to David—who was now lying on the bed with the sheet just barely covering him—she felt shy again, approaching the bed uncertainly. But as soon as he took her hand and pulled her down on top of him, her shyness evaporated as if it had never been.

His kiss was open, wet and hungry. His hands were hot and seeking as they lifted her gown and cupped her bottom, nestling her close. And when she felt his arousal beneath her, her blood zinged through her veins.

She closed her eyes and gave herself up to the sensations pummeling her. Their lovemaking was swift, urgent and thrilling. Rachel loved knowing how much he wanted her and that she alone was bringing him so much pleasure. When he cried out at the moment of climax, she felt triumphant and powerful, and she gloried in the feelings.

Afterward, he gently rolled her over and held her close. "It's a good thing you finally woke up." He kissed the tip of her nose. "Sitting there, watching you sleep, I wanted you so much, I wasn't sure I could last much longer."

Rachel laughed.

"It's not funny," he said, pretending to be serious. "I was in pain."

"You poor baby," she teased, loving his playful mood. "Do you feel better now?"

"Yes, but you'd better be warned. My condition is chronic. I figure I'll be suffering from it a lot!"

Rachel smothered a giggle. "Oh, dear, that *does* sound serious. Well, in that case, I wonder what we can do about it...."

Nuzzling her neck, he made a sound like a growl. "I know *exactly* what we can do about it."

Pretending to punch him, Rachel twisted out of his embrace. She laughed when he grabbed for her, easily evading him. "Stop that! I'm starving. Isn't it time for breakfast?"

"You mean you'd rather eat than make love?"

Rachel rolled her eyes. "Right now? Yes."

With an exaggerated sigh, he shook his head and stood. "Well, okay, if that's what you want..." The sheet slid down.

Rachel stared at him. *Oh, my.* David in clothes was sexy and handsome. David naked was just plain gorgeous. She couldn't tear her eyes away from his body, and realized it was the first time she'd actually looked at him—*really* looked at him.

Maybe she *would* rather make love again.

His voice was husky. "Like what you see?"

Rachel cleared her throat and slowly raised her eyes to his. "Yes," she murmured. "Very much."

He smiled, walking slowly toward her. "Sure you won't change your mind about what you're hungry for?"

She swallowed.

"I thought so," he said.

The next thing she knew they were both in the shower. Later, spent and limp and dazed with pleasure, she stood in David's arms, the hot water cascading over them, and Rachel thought if she died right then, it wouldn't matter, because she would die happier than any woman had any right to be.

That afternoon they flew to Colombé. As their plane began its gradual descent and the island came into sharper focus, Rachel decided it was the most beautiful place she'd ever seen. It was so beautiful, it didn't seem real. The aquamarine sea, the pristine white beaches, the lush emerald hills dotted with red-tile-roofed houses, and the brilliant sun washing everything in gold.

If only she had her paints with her! *Oh, sure. As if you could paint. That would be a dead giveaway that you're not who you pretend to be.* Well, maybe that *had* been a ridiculous thought. At the very least, Rachel promised herself, she would buy a couple of those throwaway cameras and take lots of pictures. Although painting from photographs wasn't her favorite way to re-create something, it wasn't impossible.

After landing, they were met by a young islander who introduced himself as Ben. He helped David carry their luggage to a bright yellow Jeep. Soon they were on their way, driving first through the touristy downtown area and then along a curving road that paralleled the sea. Rachel breathed deeply. The air was balmy and scented with the fragrance of thousands of flowers. Rachel loved flowers, and these were a veritable feast for the senses. Bougainvillea, orchids, jasmine, fuchsia, oleander, hibiscus—there were so many, Rachel had a hard time identifying them all. The colors were amazing. Scarlets and pinks and purples and yellows and whites and oranges—a dizzying and ever-changing kaleidoscope. Ideas for several possible paintings began to simmer.

"So what do you think?" David said.

Rachel sighed. "I love it. It's perfect."

He smiled with pleasure. "Wait'll you see the villa. It's coming up, right around this next bend." He pointed. "There it is."

"Oh, it's lovely."

Built on a small promontory, it was pale pink stucco with the de rigueur red tile roof. Although from this angle it seemed to be surrounded by thick foliage, she imagined that the sea side would have a magnificent view.

It did.

Rachel stood on the back terrace and gazed out to sea, which glittered so brightly under the late-afternoon sun it almost hurt her eyes to look at it.

The villa was the perfect size for two people, she decided later. It had a large, L-shaped living room, a fully stocked kitchen, a separate dining room, a huge bathroom with an enormous raised tub, and an equally enormous bedroom with French doors that opened onto their own secluded beach. "Wonderful," she murmured, imagining lying in bed listening to the sound of the surf.

David slid his hand around her waist and squeezed. She smiled into his eyes and saw the promise there. Her heart gave a little hop.

A week. A whole week, alone here in this beautiful place, with David.

What more could anyone ask for?

And so their honeymoon began. The first two days were lazy and sun filled. They kept mostly to themselves, swimming, eating, sleeping and making love. Rachel had never imagined it was possible to be so happy.

David was the perfect man. The perfect companion. And the perfect lover.

She blushed every time she thought about their lovemaking. David made her feel things, *want* things she'd never imagined she could feel or want. She'd never even dreamed that feelings like hers were possible, let alone attainable.

In just a couple of days it had gotten so that all she had to do was think about him making love to her, and she would want him. And she was no longer at all shy about showing him how much she wanted him, either. In fact, the night before, she'd initiated their lovemaking, walking up behind him and sliding her hands around to stroke him. His arousal was immediate and flattering.

Within minutes they were frantically tearing off their clothes. They didn't even make it to the bed.

Afterward, David picked her up from the floor and carried her to the bed, where they lay in each other's arms and talked, which Rachel liked almost as much as she liked making love.

David idly stroked her breast, his lips pressed against her forehead. "I knew it would be this way between us," he said.

"What way?" Rachel said lazily. She loved it when he touched her. She didn't think she'd ever get tired of it.

"You know what way," he said gruffly. He stopped stroking and bent to take the nipple into his mouth. He sucked hard, then gently bit, and amazingly, incredibly, desire arrowed through her again. This time, when he pushed deep inside her, he looked down into her eyes. "I knew it would be *this* way," he said. "Not ever getting enough of each other. Wanting each other all the time." He moved slowly, pushing deeper and deeper. "You *do* want me, don't you?"

"More than life itself," she said, opening her mouth to his as her body fell apart around him.

"Today we're going parasailing," David announced on the morning of the third day.

Rachel gulped. She was terrified of parasailing, but Roxanne loved it. "Parasailing?"

He frowned. "What's wrong? Don't you want to?"

"I, um..." *Oh, great! Now what?* "The last time I

went parasailing, I got really sick.'' She couldn't go parasailing. If he saw her parasailing, he would know immediately that she wasn't Roxanne.

His frown deepened. ''When was that?''

''It was back in April. You were out of town on a business trip,'' Rachel said desperately.

''Well, if you don't want to, I could cancel, I guess. Hell, I don't care if we do anything.'' He grinned. ''I was just thinking about what would make *you* happy.''

Relief made Rachel feel weak. ''I *am* happy,'' she said. ''Right now I'm the happiest woman in the world.''

''Does Rachel know where we're staying?'' David said later that day.

The question jolted Rachel, coming as it did from out of the blue while she and David were having a leisurely lunch on the veranda of one of the town's hotels. ''Yes, she does.''

''Maybe she'll call you here, then.''

''I don't think so.'' She evaded his eyes.

''Why not?''

''I, uh, don't think she'd want to disturb us on our honeymoon.'' She finally looked up.

David took a bite of his red snapper and nodded. ''You're probably right. Rachel's pretty thoughtful that way.''

Rachel looked down at her plate again to hide the guilt she was sure shone in her eyes for all the world to see.

"Your father sure was ticked off about her leaving like that," David continued.

"Yes." Rachel forced herself to eat a small bite of rice and battled to get herself under control.

"Wonder if he'd have been as mad if it had been you who'd pulled something like that."

Rachel swallowed. "I've wondered that myself," she said truthfully, meeting his quizzical gaze as evenly as she could.

David ate some more fish and buttered another roll. He took a bite. His dark eyes were thoughtful. "Does it bother you?"

"Does what bother me?"

"Knowing you've always been your father's favorite?"

Rachel couldn't think how to answer his question. She had no idea how Roxanne felt about the subject. Although they'd had few secrets from one another, their father and his obvious preference for Roxanne had been studiously avoided by both twins. She finally decided she would answer his question according to her own feelings. "Yes. It bothers me."

"It's a damned shame, I think, his attitude about Rachel."

"He probably can't help how he feels. Don't they say that parents usually *do* have a favorite? It doesn't mean they don't love their other children as much, just that maybe they can't relate to them as well." Rachel had told herself this so many times, she could say it easily. "I mean, you know, Daddy's so *different* from her."

"Have you ever tried to talk to him about it?"

Rachel shook her head.

"Maybe you should."

There was something about his expression that confused Rachel. Something almost...accusatory. Could that possibly be? Could David be thinking something *negative* about Roxanne? The idea brought a burst of happiness. "Don't you think Rachel is the one who should talk to Daddy?" she said slowly.

"Yeah, I'd like to see her stick up for herself and quit letting your father put her down the way he does, but I also think *you* should—" Abruptly, he broke off. "Nope. Sorry. I shouldn't be telling you what to do. This is none of my business."

"Of course it's your business."

He shook his head. "No, it's not. Your relationship with your sister and your father is yours, just as my relationship with my grandmother is mine."

With every word, David's integrity and basic decency was reinforced. With every word, Rachel felt a little smaller than she'd felt before.

Oh, David, how I hope you won't hate me. How I hope someday you'll understand.

For a while they ate in silence. Then, just as David finished his meal, he said, "You know, it really is unlike Rachel to have just left like that."

Rachel had hoped they'd exhausted the subject of her supposed defection, at least for now. She sighed.

"Yes, but the way things happened, she really didn't have much of a choice."

"Why didn't she?"

"Well, I didn't tell Daddy this, but Carlos came to the church and...and he begged her to come with him. I mean, he was virtually on his way out of town when he decided he couldn't leave without her. And, you know, the wedding was going to start in just minutes, and she didn't want—"

"I understand all that. But she still could have come out and at least *spoken* to your father," David insisted. "It would have been the right thing to do."

"She didn't want to upset him right before the wedding."

"That doesn't make sense."

No, of course it didn't make sense, Rachel thought glumly, because "Rachel" had upset her father right before the wedding, anyway. "I guess she wasn't thinking straight. It...it was such an emotional moment and Carlos was insisting she leave with him right then."

"He sounds like a jerk."

Rachel hadn't thought she could feel any worse than she already did, but the more David talked, the more miserable she became. "He's not a jerk, David. He's really a nice guy. I think he was just scared he'd lose her. You know, afraid if he didn't get—" she swallowed "—Rachel...to go with him then, she would never go. That maybe, if she went out to talk to Daddy, he would somehow talk her out of going."

David seemed about to say something else, then shrugged. "Yeah, I'm sure you're right. I just...I don't know, she's always been such a straight shooter, this just surprised me."

Straight shooter. Oh, God.

"Do you think they've gotten married?"

Rachel tried to smile, but was afraid her effort was less than satisfactory. "Yes, I—I think they probably have."

"Well..." He reached across the table to take her hand. "In that case, I hope she's happy. Hell, if they're even half as happy as we are, then Carlos is a lucky man." He picked up her hand and kissed the back of it.

As always, his touch filled her with a deep joy. But along with the joy was an underlying ache, a harbinger of the inevitable pain to come.

It doesn't matter. You can stand the pain. Being with David like this is worth any amount of suffering.

"I love you," he said softly, smiling into her eyes.

"I love you, too," she answered around the lump in her throat.

He leaned forward, murmuring against her ear. "Let's go back to our cabana." His voice was a throaty chuckle. "I feel that chronic condition acting up again." To emphasize, he nuzzled her ear, letting the tip of his tongue touch the sensitive inner skin.

Desire curled deep as her breathing quickened. Wordlessly, she nodded.

David reached into his pocket and threw a couple of twenty-dollar bills on the table, then, hand in hand, they walked off together.

Chapter Seven

David was happier than he'd ever thought he could be. Roxanne was amazing, he decided, watching her as she searched for shells. He admired the way her white bikini—which barely covered her curves—offset her tan. She was one of those lucky women who rarely burned. She'd already had a light tan when they'd arrived on the island, but now, after four days of sun, it had deepened to an even golden brown.

She was also a woman whose moods seemed to effortlessly adapt to his. He couldn't believe he'd ever worried about making her happy. She was obviously as deeply happy and contented as he was. He could see that happiness and contentment in everything she said and did, in every look and touch.

And most satisfying of all, she was no longer jittery and always having to be doing something exciting. She was calm and relaxed, just as contented to do something quiet like collect shells or stroll the beach or sit outside in the privacy of their little patio as she was to dance at the hotel or one of the small clubs in town or gamble in the casino, which they had done the previous evening.

This newly revealed ability to be quiet, to just sit and think or enjoy the beauty of the surrounding scenery, reminded him of Rachel.

Roxanne and Rachel were much more alike than he'd ever realized, he guessed. Rachel's running off the way she had proved she was just as adventurous and daring as Roxanne, and these past few days showed that Roxanne could be just as contented and low-key as Rachel.

He wondered how Rachel was doing. Roxanne was probably right—Rachel and Carlos were no doubt married by now. In fact, David imagined that when he and Roxanne got back to Houston, Rachel would have contacted her father and told him the news.

Maybe in a month or so he and Roxanne could go visit Rachel and her new husband. He still had plenty of vacation time accumulated, and Roxanne was her own boss, so she could easily get away.

He smiled, letting the hot sand run through his fingers while he continued to think and watch Roxanne, who now stood in the surf, toeing the wet sand beneath her feet. As he watched, she bent to extract a shell from the sand and he admired the way her bikini bottom stretched taut over her behind. Even that unconscious motion caused his body to stir. Just then, she looked around. He smiled, and she smiled back, then slowly walked toward him.

"What were you thinking about just now?" She sank down next to him.

"Would you believe world peace?"

"Nope." Her eyes were brilliant in the morning sun. She leaned over to kiss him. She tasted warm and sweet, like sunshine and flowers. "Not that I think you don't *ever* think about world peace, but somehow that doesn't seem like a subject that would overly concern you right now." She stretched out on the beach blanket.

"You're right." He turned slightly, laying his hand on her warm thigh. Lazily, he stroked the silky skin. "I was thinking about Rachel."

"What about Rachel?"

He smiled, slowly inching his hand upward. "I was thinking how much more alike the two of you are than I ever imagined."

She shaded her eyes from the sun as she met his gaze. "Are we?"

"Uh-huh." Now he caressed the soft flesh of her inner thigh.

"What else were you thinking?"

"I was hoping she's happy."

"Oh, I'm sure she's h-happy."

Her breath caught a little on the last word, because

while she was talking he'd slid his fingers under the tiny piece of material that served as the bottom of her bikini. He caressed her, watching the way her eyes drifted shut, the way she arched her back and the way her nipples grew more pronounced under her snug-fitting top.

"David..." The word floated on a sigh.

"What?" he said huskily.

Her throat worked. "S-someone might see." But her protest was weak, and she didn't try to push his hand away when he tugged her bikini bottom down.

"Then let's go inside," he murmured, leaning over and kissing her warm belly while his fingers continued to stroke, then probe, finding her already wet and ready.

"You're insatiable." Her voice was thready with the desire that was never far from the surface now.

"Do you want me to stop?"

She squeezed her eyes shut. "No, no..."

He kissed her then, deeply.

"Do you want me?"

"Yes," she gasped.

"Then open your eyes. I want to see your eyes."

He loved looking at her when she was nearing a climax. He loved knowing he'd put that glazed expression on her face, that he'd made her crazy with wanting him, just as he was crazy with wanting her, and that if he took her now, right out here on the beach, she would let him.

"Now?" He could barely get the word out.

"Yes, yes, now, now...." She touched him then, and he groaned. He pulled her up, and within seconds they'd tugged off their bathing suits and, hand in hand, raced into the sea. And there, barely covered by the foaming surf, he plunged into her again and again until they both cried out in an agony of pleasure so intense all David could do was hold on to her and hope he didn't die from it.

How many times had they made love since the wedding? Rachel wondered. So many she had lost count. At least twice every day, and sometimes three or four times. She was still thinking about the incredible interlude on the beach that morning, made all the more deliciously exciting by the forbidden element of making love right out there in the open, where somebody *could* see them.

But, oh, it had been thrilling, and she'd loved every minute of it.

Afterward, David had said, "If we keep this up, I'm going to have a heart attack before we leave this place." But then he'd laughed and added, "But what a way to go."

This morning at the beach hadn't been the first lovemaking session of the day, either. They'd made love when they first woke up, so it was already twice today, and it was only midafternoon.

And, of course, there was tonight....

Rachel sighed dreamily, thinking about tonight. Maybe they would fill the tub and take a bath together.

Rachel loved that. There was something decadent and wicked and totally wonderful about sitting nestled up against David in a tub filled with hot, bath-oil-scented water and feeling his arousal against her bottom while his hands—those magical hands—soaped her.

That's what they'd done their second night on the island. And they'd done it by candlelight, with music playing in the background and the windows open to the night breeze. Even now, remembering, Rachel's breath quickened.

What was *wrong* with her?

She could hardly believe this...this wanton creature she'd become.

She knew she should be embarrassed by the uninhibited sexuality David had unleashed in her, and by all the things they'd done together, but she wasn't.

She was reveling in it.

She loved sex with David. More, she loved knowing she was responsible for bringing him to such peaks of need and pleasure, that all she had to do was look at him in a certain way, and he would want her.

Yes, that was it. That was it!

When they were making love, it was *her* he wanted. Not Roxanne.

Her—Rachel.

That was why she felt no shame and no guilt.

Of course, he thinks you're Roxanne....

Angrily she pushed the thought away.

No.

She would not spoil what she had right now. No

matter who he thought he'd married, she was the one he'd been making love with, and she was the one he wanted morning, noon and night.

The realization made her heart soar.

Maybe, when he found out she wasn't Roxanne, he wouldn't care!

Careful, careful, don't start wishing for the impossible. You'll just end up getting hurt.

But it was hard not to, especially in light of the fact that she knew David was just as happy as she was.

She glanced at him now. They had been strolling along Colombé's main street, but David had stopped to look into the window of a shop that sold silver jewelry.

"Look at that," he said now, pointing to a delicate bracelet inlaid with dozens of red coral stones. "Do you like it?"

"I love it." She smiled. "It matches my dress." Today she was wearing one of the half-dozen sundresses Roxanne had packed. Rachel particularly liked this one, with its crisscross straps front and back and its soft, floaty material.

"Let's go in, then. I want to get it for you."

They had turned to enter the shop when, from behind Rachel, a female voice called out. "Roxanne!"

Rachel's heart leapt into her throat and she stopped dead.

"Roxanne!" the woman said again, closer this time.

Slowly, fighting the panic that threatened to overwhelm her, Rachel turned.

The woman was blond, young, pretty. She wore a hot pink sunsuit and strappy sandals and had a bright smile and eyes. She was obviously delighted to see Rachel, and waved as she walked forward.

Rachel had no idea who she was.

"Hi," she said, reaching Rachel and David. "Gosh, it's great to see you again!"

"H-hi," Rachel managed, even though her mind was spinning.

The blonde continued to chatter gaily, saying, "How long has it been? Two years? Three? Gee, you look *terrific*, Roxanne. Of course, you always *did*. I *love* that dress you're wearing. Red is definitely your color." Without pausing for breath, she added, "What are you doing here?"

"I, um..."

The blonde gave Rachel a quizzical smile. "You don't remember me, do you?"

"No, I'm sorry, I—"

"Oh, it's okay," the blonde said. "I know I look different." She grinned. "I dyed my hair. It used to be dark brown. And my contacts are a darker green than my natural color. I'm Marlo. Marlo French."

Rachel thought hard, even as she said, "Marlo, hi, you're right, the hair *does* make a difference." With a rush of intense relief, she remembered how, several years ago, Roxanne had mentioned a Marlo that she'd met at a fashion conference.

But try as she might, Rachel couldn't remember anything Roxanne had said about the woman except that she kind of looked like Marlo Thomas and that they'd hung around together throughout the conference.

"It's great to see you again, too," she said. Why hadn't she paid closer attention to Roxanne when she'd talked about Marlo?

Marlo looked pointedly at David.

Rachel turned to him, still struggling for calm. "Marlo, this is my h-husband...." *You idiot! Chill out or she'll wonder what's wrong with you!* "David Hanson. David, darling, this is Marlo French. We met a few years ago at a conference in New York."

"Husband, huh?" Marlo said. She stuck out her hand. "It's nice to meet you, David."

David smiled, saying, "Nice to meet you, too." They shook hands.

Marlo said, "So, what are you two doing here? Is this a vacation?"

David's smile expanded, his eyes glowing with pride. He put his arm possessively around Rachel's waist. "We're on our honeymoon."

Rachel's mind spun frantically. She prayed Marlo wouldn't ask anything or refer to anything Rachel couldn't answer.

"Well, it's a great place for it," Marlo said. "Where are you staying?"

"We rented a villa out on the west side of the island."

"We're at the Palm Breeze." She looked around. "Kenny, he's my boyfriend, he's here someplace."

She shaded her eyes and stood on tiptoe. "Oh, there he is! Kenny! *Ken-neee.* Oh, darn. He can't hear me." She turned back to face them, her face a picture of disappointment. "And I really wanted you to meet him."

Oh, God, Rachel thought. *What am I going to do? She's obviously not going to go away.*

"So, how long are you guys here for?"

"We'll be here another four days," David said.

"Tonight's our last night," Marlo said. But before Rachel could feel any relief about her imminent departure, she added, "Say, if you guys aren't busy tonight, why don't the four of us get together for dinner?" Her voice was eager. "That way Roxanne and I can get all caught up, and you guys can meet Kenny."

Although spending an evening dodging bullets and praying she would escape unscathed was the last thing Rachel wanted to do, how could she say no? What possible excuse could she give? Roxanne wouldn't have declined the invitation. She loved being with her friends. She would have been delighted to see Marlo again and wouldn't have considered her company an imposition.

Resigned, Rachel looked at David and smiled. "That sounds like fun, doesn't it?"

The evening was excruciating.

Rachel couldn't let her guard down for one minute. She felt as if she were in the middle of a minefield and at any moment might take a wrong step and have everything blow up in her face.

Thank goodness, though, Marlo was the talkative kind of person who seemed content with nods and smiles from Rachel rather than any kind of more concrete input.

And Kenny was also a talker. A big bear of a man with unruly dark auburn hair and guileless blue eyes, he was an amiable extrovert who seemed to consider it his mission in life to keep them laughing and entertained.

And if Rachel hadn't been so terrified of exposure, she would have enjoyed him tremendously. Both of them, actually. Marlo was a nice woman and easy to be around.

"So, how long have you two been together?" she asked now, smiling across the table at Rachel and David.

"Roxanne and I have known each other since we were little kids," David said. He put his arm around Rachel, unabashedly kissing her cheek. "And I've loved her forever."

Suddenly the enormity of what she had done...of how she was deceiving all of these people...especially David, dearest David, hit Rachel like a blast of icy air. She could hardly look at Marlo and Kenny. She knew she had to say something, but no words would come. *You're a liar and a miserable excuse for a human being.*

"It took me a while to persuade her to marry me, though," David continued.

Marlo grinned. "Some women just like playing hard to get."

"Is that what you were doing?" David teased.

Rachel looked up. Saw the tenderness in his eyes. The smile on his beloved face. She swallowed, fighting the tears that hovered so alarmingly close. And then, from somewhere, the right words came. Afterward, she wasn't sure how she'd had the nerve to say them, especially in front of strangers. All she knew was that it was important to be honest.

"I don't know. What I do know is that that person, the one who kept you guessing for so long, is gone, for good, and this person—" she touched her heart "—thinks you're the best husband any woman could ever want." Her voice trembled. "I—I can't imagine what it would be like to live without you."

"Aw," Marlo said. She smiled wistfully. "Isn't that sweet?" When Kenny didn't answer, she poked him. "Isn't that sweet, Kenny?"

He grinned sheepishly.

David only smiled, telling her with his eyes how much her words had meant to him.

Later, as the combo began to warm up in preparation for the evening's dancing, Rachel thought about feigning some kind of illness so she and David could leave, but quickly discarded the idea.

If she did that, she would have to continue to pretend when she and David got back to the villa, and she didn't want to add yet another lie to the ones she was already committed to carrying out.

"Oh, goody," Marlo said. "We love to dance."

"*You* love to dance," Kenny said. "I have two left feet."

David laughed. "Roxanne loves to dance, too."

Rachel had no choice but to smile. Oh, well, she thought. If they were dancing, they wouldn't have to talk to Marlo and Kenny, and there would be no danger of exposure. Still, it was hard for Rachel to relax, even though normally she adored dancing with David.

He noticed. "Is something wrong, sweetheart?" he said as they moved to the sinuous beat of a rumba. "You're awfully quiet."

"No," Rachel said quickly. "Nothing's wrong. I'm just a little tired." Surely it was safe to say she was tired.

"Even after that nap we had?"

She forced a lighthearted chuckle. "Nap! Some nap. That's the problem. You're wearing me out."

He pulled her closer. "Are you complaining?"

"No. No, I'm not complaining."

"Good thing, 'cause even if you were, you're stuck with me." Smiling, he added, "C'mon. Let's go tell Marlo and Kenny goodbye. I'm starting to feel a little tired myself."

Something *was* wrong.

David knew it, even though she'd denied it, but he couldn't figure out what it was. She'd been tense all night. He watched her as she said goodbye to Marlo and Kenny, trying to pinpoint exactly what the problem might be, but for the life of him, he couldn't.

As he and Roxanne walked slowly out to the taxi stand, he said casually, "I thought tonight was nice, didn't you?"

"Uh-huh."

"Marlo's sure a lot of fun."

"Yes, she is."

"Did it bother you that we ran into them?"

"Bother me? Why should it bother me?"

David didn't know, but he was more sure than ever that something about Marlo and Kenny *had* bothered Roxanne. He could hear it in her voice, no matter what she said. "Well," he said lightly, "I was flattering myself that maybe you just wanted to be alone with me."

She laughed, and there was an undercurrent of relief in her voice as she answered. "Oh, David, I thought you'd think I was silly, but that's exactly it. Our...our honeymoon is ours, and I hated sharing it, even with people as nice as Marlo and Kenny."

He thought about challenging her. Continuing to probe until he got to the real truth, but then he thought, oh, what the hell. Whatever was bothering her was over now, and it probably wasn't important, anyway. Why make a big deal out of it? Instead, he pulled her closer and kissed her temple, saying softly, "Well, we'll be alone soon."

Twenty minutes later, as they walked onto their terrace, he drew her into his arms. For a long time they stood there in the moonlight, arms wrapped around each other, and kissed.

Later, after they'd made love and were lying in each other's arms, he thought again how glad he was they'd waited until they were married to become intimate, because how would he have stood it if they hadn't? If they'd been lovers before, he'd never have been able to wait so long before marrying her, not the way he felt about her now. "You were right, you know," he said softly, tracing the line of her jaw.

"About what?"

He explained what he'd been thinking, fully expecting she would agree with him. But she made no comment, which kind of disappointed him. In fact, she was quiet for so long, he began to be concerned.

Finally he said, "Sweetheart, I know something's bothering you."

She sighed deeply.

"Tell me what it is," he coaxed.

Her eyes were dark, shining pools as they met his. "I was thinking how very much I love you. So much that it frightens me."

He tightened his arms around her. "Why should it frighten you?"

She didn't answer for a long time. Then, finally, in a low voice tinged with sadness, she said, "Because it will be so hard to bear if...if I should ever lose you."

"You'll never lose me," he said gruffly. He cupped

her chin, lifting her face so he could look into her eyes again. "You're stuck with me forever."

She nodded, even smiled, but there was a suspicious sheen in her eyes.

Touched by her intensity, he kissed her tenderly. "You couldn't get rid of me if you tried."

How *was* she going to bear it? Rachel wondered. How was she going to give him up? She drew circles in the sand and watched him, marveling at the beauty of his body. He was sitting on a big bath towel, doing sit-ups in the shade of a nearby palm tree. It was the morning of their next to last day in St. John. Tomorrow at noon they would leave, and for Rachel it would be the beginning of the end.

How was she going to tell him?

When was she going to tell him?

Not on the plane, certainly, for all the reasons she hadn't told him on the plane coming here.

The plan was for them to go directly from the airport to David's house. That was it, then. She would tell him when they were in the privacy of his home, and then, afterward, she would leave.

She closed her eyes, fighting tears.

Leave him.

How could she bear it?

Never to see him again. Never to touch him again. Never to kiss him. Never to feel him touching her.

Oh, God...

"Sweetheart?"

Rachel jumped. Swallowed.

David dropped to the sand beside her. His chest and arms were covered by a fine sheen of moisture. He smelled of sun and suntan oil and sweat. His dark eyes shone with concern. "Why so sad?"

Rachel shrugged, fighting to control her emotions. "I guess because I hate to leave here."

He kissed her shoulder. "I know. Me, too."

"I wish...I wish we could stay here forever. That we never had to go back to the real world."

"Why don't we? We can quit our jobs, and I'll sell my house and you and Rachel can sell your town house. Shoot, we could even sell our cars. No need for a car here. We'll pool our money and buy one of those little houses up in the hills."

If only it was that easy. If only it was possible to hide out forever. The lump in her throat felt as big as a grapefruit and refused to go away.

"Hey," he said, sliding his arm around her waist and kissing her cheek, "c'mon. Cheer up. Maybe it won't be Colombé, but you'll enjoy getting the house fixed up and starting our lives together at home."

Rachel tried to smile, but the pain of knowing that instead of starting life as a married couple they would be ending their time together was too acute.

"It's not like we can't come back to Colombé," he said tenderly. "In fact, we can come back for our first anniversary." When she didn't answer, he tipped her face up. "Now, come on, smile."

Rachel knew that years from now, when she thought back to this moment, it would be remembered as the day her heart began to break.

Chapter Eight

That night their lovemaking was bittersweet. Rachel poured her heart and soul into it, trying to show David by her intensity how much he meant to her. She wanted him to always remember this last night on Colombé, no matter what happened next.

Afterward, as if on some level he knew what she felt, he cradled her close and said, "I'll never forget this week."

"I won't, either," she said softly. "It's been wonderful." If only she could stay here, in the warm circle of his arms, always. If only they never had to go back to Houston.

"We're going to have the best life together," he continued. He lifted her chin and kissed her, letting his mouth linger softly against hers.

David, my darling...

Tucking her head under his chin again, he said, "You know what I'm looking forward to?"

"What?"

"I can't wait till we have kids."

Rachel's heart knocked painfully.

"I'd like to have at least three. I always hated being an only child."

"Did you?"

"Uh-huh. I envied you and Rachel because you had each other, and you always seemed so close."

"Were you lonely, David?"

"Yes. My grandmother tried hard. She always had kids around for me to play with, and she took me all kinds of places, but there were times, you know, when the other kids' parents came to school parties or plays. And I remember once, in the fifth grade, when different fathers came and talked about what they did for a living. Even the kids whose parents were divorced had fathers, and they'd be so excited when it was *their* father up there talking to the rest of us...so proud...." His voice trailed off.

For a long moment he was silent, and Rachel's heart ached for that little boy.

Then, in a brisker tone, he said, "It doesn't matter anymore. I survived." He kissed her forehead. "Anyway, now I've got you, and we're going to have a family of our own."

She and David were more alike than she'd known, she realized, for even though she'd had Roxanne, there had been so many times Rachel had been lonely, too. "I think three is a perfect number," she whispered.

He placed his hand on her belly. "You could be pregnant now."

Rachel swallowed. "Yes."

She could feel his smile against her forehead. "I hope you are."

All she could do was nod, because she didn't trust herself to speak.

"I hope we have a little girl first. A beautiful little girl. Someone who would grow up to be just like you."

Rachel's eyes filled with tears. "Oh, David," she said brokenly.

"Hey, what's with all these tears?" He wiped them away with his hand, then kissed her tenderly. "You still sad about leaving tomorrow?"

"It's not that, it's...you're so good to me. I don't deserve it."

"What are you talking about?" He pulled back a little, and when she avoided his eyes, he tipped her chin up so he could look at her. "What do you mean, you don't *deserve* it? You're my wife, and I love you. Why wouldn't I be good to you? You're good to *me*."

Every word was like another nail being pounded into her coffin. "I *don't* deserve it. I—I'm not the person you think I am."

He laughed, the sound affectionate and indulgent. "That's crazy. You're exactly the person I want you to be. You know, it's a funny thing. How many years have I known you? You'd think I'd know everything about you. Well, this week I've discovered things about you, parts of your personality that I never saw before, and they've made me love you even more."

"Oh, David. Do you...do you really mean that?"

"Hell, yes, I mean it. Now, will you stop this?"

She could hear the beginnings of exasperation in his voice and knew she had to either tell him the truth now or set his mind at ease by lightening up. She touched his cheek. "David?"

"What?"

"Thank you."

"For *what?*"

"For saying what you did. I—I'll never forget it."

He captured her hand and, bringing it to his mouth, kissed the open palm. "Damn right you won't forget it, because I intend to remind you of it every day for the rest of our lives."

The following afternoon, sitting next to David in the first-class section of their flight from Colombé to Miami, Rachel looked out the window and thought about that conversation. She should have told him then. Regardless of the fact that she wanted to wait until they were in Houston, she should have told him then. But selfishly, she hadn't wanted to relinquish those last precious hours, so she'd said nothing.

You deserve every awful thing David is going to think of you, you know that, don't you, because last night you weren't thinking of him and his welfare, you were thinking of yourself!

She'd had the perfect opening. When he'd said how she'd shown him personality traits he'd never seen before, she should have said, straight out, "That's because I'm not Roxanne. I'm Rachel."

Oh, God.

Each mile brought her closer to the time when she would have to say just that.

She couldn't even imagine what he would say when she finally got the words out. How he would feel. That he would despise her was a given. That he would probably order her out of his house and his life and that he would probably refuse to ever see her or speak to her again was a distinct possibility.

She tried to be stoic as she pictured the scenario. She reminded herself over and over again that it had been worth it. That she would not trade the past week for anything. That the joy she'd experienced with David was worth all the pain and loneliness, and every bit of the heartache and misery she was going to feel.

"'Tis better to have loved and lost than never to have loved at all."

Tennyson had written those words. And Rachel believed in their truth. But there was no use kidding herself. It was going to be hard.

And it was going to hurt so much more than she'd ever imagined, because until she'd spent this time with David, until she'd experienced actually *being* with him, she'd had no real understanding of how much he really meant to her.

Sure, she'd loved him, but now…now he was as essential to her as the air she breathed.

He was *part* of her.

Without him, she would not be whole. Without him, a piece of her heart, a piece of her soul, would be gone forever.

Please, God, please, God, let me be pregnant. Let me have a part of David to keep and to love. Over and over, she silently repeated her prayer.

And then, because she could no longer endure thinking about what awaited her at home, she closed her eyes and willed herself to sleep.

David was glad Roxanne had finally fallen asleep, because he knew she must be tired. She'd slept fitfully last night, and there were dark shadows under her eyes today.

He frowned.

Why was she so reluctant to go home?

She acted as if something had spooked her, but he had no idea what it could be. And why had she acted so strange last night, saying all those crazy things about not being the person he thought she was? It was almost as if she were hiding some terrible secret, but that was nutty.

Hell, he'd known her and Rachel all of their lives. There wasn't anything he didn't know about them and their family.

That's not true. You said yourself that this week you'd discovered all kinds of things about Roxanne that you hadn't known before.

Well, sure, but discovering hidden facets to someone's personality was a hell of a lot different than discovering some family skeleton. After all, no one was an open book. He was a perfect example. He'd be willing to bet his grandmother thought she knew everything about him and his personality, but she didn't. He'd been hiding his secret dreams for years. Everyone hid *something.*

His frown deepened.

What was Roxanne hiding?

Obviously, it had something to do with returning to Houston, because she had not seemed the least worried or unhappy at the beginning of the week, when they'd first arrived in Colombé. Her fears or worries or whatever they were had begun to show themselves only in the past two days, as they prepared to go home.

And now she looked tired and tense again, just the way she had in the weeks before their wedding.

The thought bothered him.

It bothered him a lot.

He sure hoped returning to Houston wasn't going to bring about a resumption of that almost frenetic behavior she'd exhibited then, because he liked the Roxanne he'd discovered in Colombé better than he'd liked the old Roxanne.

Much better.

And he didn't want to lose her.

* * *

Instead of the forty-five-minute wait they'd expected to have in Miami, their flight to Houston was delayed because of bad weather and took off four hours late. So it was after midnight when their taxi pulled in to the driveway of the small West University house David had purchased six months earlier.

By the time they arrived, Rachel was completely worn out, physically as well as mentally. The long hours in the air, the waiting and the worrying she'd done had taken their toll.

She knew there was no way she could face the emotional confrontation of telling David the truth. Not tonight. Besides, he was tired, too, she could see that plainly, and he had to go into the office in the morning.

Her confession would have to wait until tomorrow, she told herself. Decision made, she couldn't help feeling relieved, even though her reprieve would be shortlived.

"Let's not even bother to unpack," David said, unceremoniously dumping their suitcases in a corner of the bedroom. "I'm beat, and I know you are. Let's just go to bed."

Rachel nodded gratefully.

That night, for the first time since the wedding, they did not make love. And for this, too, Rachel was grateful. She had already said her physical goodbye to David in Colombé. Making love again would only have made it more painful to tell him the truth tomorrow.

* * *

They slept through the alarm the next morning.

"Damn!" David said, jumping out of bed. "It's seven-thirty!"

There was no time for breakfast or anything else before he had to leave for the office.

"I'll grab a cup of coffee on the way," he said, giving her a hurried kiss goodbye. "Don't worry about dinner. I know you've probably got a busy day today, too. We can send out for Chinese or something. And afterward, we can go over to the town house and finish moving your things over, okay?"

"All right."

"Call you later," he said. Then, grinning, he kissed her again. "I like this. Having you here in the morning. Knowing you'll be here tonight."

Rachel liked it, too. And after he was gone, she tried not to dwell on how wonderful it would be to have the right to be there every day. Thinking about things that could never be was futile.

She could not change the facts. She wasn't really his wife. And she never would be.

With a leaden heart she walked back to the bedroom where she made the bed and unpacked his suitcases. Lovingly, she put his belongings away. She held his soft cotton shirts against her face, breathing in the lingering scent of David. Tears filled her eyes as she stroked the silky black pajama bottoms he'd worn on their wedding night. Even his scuffed Docksiders put a lump in her throat.

Other than finding something clean to wear, she ignored her own two suitcases. Roxanne's two suitcases, she corrected herself. There was no reason to unpack them.

She filled the washer with a load of David's laundry and set aside the clothing that needed to go to the dry cleaner's. Even though she wasn't legally David's wife, she could at least do these last wifely chores for him. She wanted to do them. They were a labor of love.

Once she'd finished with everything she could see to do at his house, she showered and dressed, then drove Roxanne's car—which she'd left in David's garage the day before the wedding—over to their town house.

Because Rachel had fully expected to be there the past week, no arrangements had been made for anyone to gather mail or the newspaper. As a result, the mailbox was overflowing, and newspapers had accumulated in the courtyard.

Inside, it gave her a pang to see the paintings propped against the walls of the dining room and her notes and sketchbooks stacked on the dining-room table. She knew that no matter how miserable she was going to feel tomorrow after unburdening herself to David, she would not be able to wallow in it. Because if she didn't immediately get to work, she would lose not only David, but this golden opportunity to further her career.

And then she'd *really* have nothing.

Determinedly putting that depressing thought out of her mind, she sorted through the mail, delaying the moment when she would have to check her telephone messages. There were the usual assortment of bills and junk mail and the promised contract from the Blythe Gallery. Continuing to postpone the inevitable, Rachel looked through the contract, then carried it into her bedroom. She wanted to read it carefully before she signed it. Finally she could delay no longer.

She pressed the message button on her recorder.

The first couple of calls were hang-ups or sales types. The third call was from Phillip Blythe's assistant, Vivian, saying she'd put Rachel's contract in the mail. "If you have any questions, just give me a call," she concluded brightly.

On the fourth call, Roxanne's voice said, "Rach? Are you there? It's me, Roxanne. Pick up if you're there. Darn. I was hoping you'd be home. Um, it's Wednesday morning, about ten o'clock. Call me as soon as you get back, okay?" She went on to give Rachel the number where she could be reached, then said, "Oh, God, Rach, I'm dying here. I have to know what happened. How Daddy took things. Is he really furious with me? I'm afraid to call him until I talk to you."

Daddy, Rachel thought. Not David. Daddy.

"I, um, wanted to know what David said, too," Roxanne's voice continued. "I hope he's okay. I—I feel bad that I stuck you with telling him. Okay, well,

I'm gonna hang up now. Talk to you later. Love you. Bye."

The phone beeped, then another message began to play. This, too, was from Roxanne. "Rach? Rach, where the devil *are* you? I've been hanging around here at Carlos's parents' house all day waiting for you to call me back. Listen, Carlos and I are getting married tomorrow morning, and then we're going to Mexico City for a short honeymoon. I'll call you when we get there, okay? I *have* to talk to you."

The next two messages were in the same vein, with Roxanne sounding more and more frustrated by her inability to raise Rachel.

The last message on the tape had been recorded the day before. "Rachel, I'm really getting worried here," Roxanne said. "Please, please call me. I'm beginning to think you don't want to talk to me. I guess if I don't hear from you by tomorrow night I'd better just bite the bullet and call Daddy anyway."

Rachel's heart lurched painfully. Dear heaven! If Roxanne called their father before Rachel had had a chance to talk to David, it would be horrible. Unthinkable. Her fingers shook as she punched in the number Roxanne had left. *Please, please be there.*

After five rings, a female answered, saying, *"Hola, hola."*

Thank goodness Rachel had had four years of Spanish. Even so, she was rusty and had to grope for the right words. *"Hola. ¿Me permite hablar con Roxanne Terraza?"*

"I am sorry," the woman said, switching to perfect English. "Roxanne has gone shopping."

"Oh," said Rachel. She bit her lip. What should she do?

"Who is calling, please?"

"I, um, I'm her sister. Could I leave a message for her, please?"

"Yes, of course. What is the message?"

"Tell her that Rachel called and that I'll call her back later. Tell her that under no circumstances is she to call Daddy or David. That's very important. She must not talk to Daddy or David. Not until she talks to me."

The woman repeated the message. "I will see that your sister receives this message as soon as she returns," she said kindly.

"Thank you," Rachel said.

"You are very welcome."

After they'd hung up, Rachel stood there, telling herself to calm down. Catastrophe had been averted. But oh, God, what if she hadn't been in time? What if Roxanne had called their father? Wouldn't that have been awful?

It didn't happen. You're safe.

But not for long, she thought miserably. Not for long.

"Hey, David, good to see you back!"

"We missed you, old man."

"Hey, man. You're lookin' good. Bein' married must agree with you, huh?"

David smiled and returned all the greetings before joining the department managers for a special meeting where they would discuss the final phase of the merger of Hanson Drilling and Carlton Oil—the physical move of Hanson to the Carlton Oil building, which was scheduled to begin the following day.

David had just settled into his seat at the head of the conference table when Carole Attley, his secretary, opened the door and poked her head inside. She looked at David. "I'm sorry, but I have to talk to you. It's important."

Her tone gave David a sense of foreboding.

"Virginia called. It's your grandmother," she said once he was outside the conference room. "She's had a heart attack." Carole put her hand on his shoulder in a gesture of comfort.

"What? When? Where is she?" He could hardly grasp what she'd said.

"She just suddenly collapsed. Virginia immediately called 911. They've taken her to St. Matthew's."

"How..." He swallowed, told himself to calm down. "How is she?"

Carole shook her head. "Virginia didn't know anything, except that she's alive."

David's heart pounded. His grandmother had always seemed so strong. So invincible. Somehow, even though he'd known better, he'd always expected her to be around. But she would be eighty on her next birthday. If she made it through this, he amended. "I'm going down there," he said. He inclined his head toward the conference room. "Tell the guys, okay? And listen, Carole, call Roxanne and tell her what's happened. Ask her if she can meet me at the hospital."

"Don't worry." Carole's eyes were sympathetic. "I'll take care of everything."

Rachel could hear the phone ringing as she unlocked the back door. Dumping the grocery bags on the kitchen table, she raced toward the cordless phone sitting on the counter. "Hello?" she said breathlessly.

"Roxanne?"

She almost said no, this is Rachel, but she caught herself in time. "Y-yes?"

"Roxanne, this is Carole."

"Carole?"

"David's secretary."

"Oh, *Carole!* I'm sorry. I must be in a fog or something. How are you?"

"I'm fine. I'm calling because David asked me to." Rachel listened with growing horror as Carole related what had happened.

"Oh, poor David," she said when Carole had finished. "Yes, of course, I'll go to the hospital immediately. And Carole, thanks for calling."

It took Rachel only ten minutes to get to St. Matthew's, which was part of the medical center complex just south of West U, where David's house was located. Parking took another five minutes. Five minutes after that found her walking out of the elevator and into the wing housing coronary care.

She saw David immediately. He and Virginia Olesky, his grandmother's longtime companion and housekeeper, were sitting together on a leather couch in the CCU waiting area. He came rushing forward to meet her.

"Oh, David, how is she?" Rachel cried, hurting for him when she saw the lines of strain.

He put his arms around her and held her close. "We don't know anything yet. God, I'm glad you're here."

She put her arms around him and closed her eyes, savoring the closeness for a few moments before he released her.

"Do you know what happened?" she asked as, arm around her, he led her over to the seating area. She smiled at the housekeeper. "Hi, Virginia."

"Hello, Roxanne."

As always, being called Roxanne gave Rachel a jolt.

"There's not much to know," David said. "She'd just finished her lunch, and she got up, walked a couple of steps and clutched her chest. Virginia was there."

Rachel looked at Virginia, whose normally cheerful countenance was creased with worry lines.

"Thank God," Virginia said. "I just keep thinking, what if I'd gone to the post office or the supermarket or something, and she'd collapsed like that, and no one had been home?"

"Well, it didn't happen, so don't think like that," Rachel said. "You *were* there."

"Yes," David said. "And you didn't panic. That's what's important." He gave Virginia a reassuring smile. Turning back to Rachel, he said, "We're waiting on Dr. Burnside now."

Rachel nodded. Elliott Burnside was the most renowned heart specialist in the city. If he was overseeing her treatment, Georgina Hanson was in good hands.

"Sit down, sweetheart," David said. "Do you want something to drink? Coffee or a Coke?"

"No, not now." Rachel sat next to Virginia and took the older woman's hand, giving it a comforting squeeze. If Georgina Hanson didn't make it, Virginia would suffer as much as David, for it was obvious to all that she cared deeply for her employer.

Virginia gave Rachel a grateful smile.

After that, the three of them did not talk much. David spent most of his time standing in front of the window at the end of the corridor, obviously too worried to sit. Rachel leafed desultorily through a dog-eared copy of *Newsweek*, and Virginia knitted. "I always carry my knitting in my purse," she explained. "It helps pass the time."

Rachel smiled. Virginia's "purse" was actually a huge canvas tote bag, and she'd never seen the older woman without it. "I don't suppose you've got any aspirin in that bag, do you?"

"As a matter of fact," Virginia said, "I do." She fished inside and produced a bottle.

"Thanks," Rachel said gratefully.

For the next hour, every time the double doors leading into the inner sanctum of the coronary care unit opened, all three of them would look up hopefully. But Dr. Burnside didn't emerge.

"What's going *on* in there?" David said after a while, giving the closed doors a thunderous look. "God, you'd think they'd come out and tell you *something.*"

"They will," Rachel said soothingly, thinking how typically male David's anger was. Women agonized and made bargains with God. Men got angry and railed.

Suddenly Rachel remembered her father. He would want to know about Georgina. He would be upset if she didn't call him. In fact, she should have called him first thing this morning. It was what Roxanne would have done.

"You know what? I just remembered," she said to David. "I should call my father."

"Of course," David said. "I forgot about him."

Rachel walked down the hall to the nurses' station, where a tiny redheaded aide directed her to the nearest pay phone. Rachel dropped in her quarter and pressed the numbers for her father's office.

"Mr. Carlton's office."

"Hi, Pilar." She took a deep breath. "Th-this is Roxanne. Is Daddy there?"

"Well, hi, sugar," his secretary of twenty-two years said. "So you're back, eh? How was it? Wonderful?"

"Yes," Rachel said. "Wonderful."

"Your daddy's on another line, but it's just one of his old poker cronies. So let me go in and do my sign language thing," Pilar said. "He'll be wantin' to talk to you, I know."

"Thanks."

"Angel!" her father's voice boomed a few minutes later. "I wondered if you were home. Was plannin' on stoppin' by later, in fact."

"Hi, Daddy," Rachel said. As always, her emotions were mixed. "I'm sorry I didn't call you earlier, but something's happened." She quickly explained.

"I'll be right there," he said when she'd finished.

"There's no reason for you to come," she said hurriedly. God, that's all she needed.

"No reason? Georgina Hanson is like family to me. Hell, she *is* family now. Of course I'm comin'." Then his voice softened. "Besides, my little girl needs me, and I'm not about to let her down."

Rachel stood by the phone for long minutes after she'd hung up. She needed to gather her strength, get herself under steely control and marshal every bit of acting talent she possessed. Because now, when David needed all the support he could get, would be a disastrous time for the truth about her to be exposed.

Five minutes later, silently telling herself she could carry out her charade for just a little while longer, she rejoined David and Virginia and settled down to wait for her father's arrival.

Chapter Nine

The combination of love and pain she always felt when she saw her father flooded Rachel as, forty-five minutes later, he walked off the elevator and headed down the hall toward her.

As always, he was nattily dressed in a tailored chocolate brown suit, pale yellow shirt and geometric print silk tie. Although Wylie Carlton was every inch a man's man—and proud of it—he took an unusual interest in clothing, a part of his personality Rachel had always considered an anomaly.

"Angel," he said, reaching her side and enveloping her in a bear hug. He kissed her cheek, smiling down at her as he released her. "I sure am glad you're home. I missed my girl."

Rachel smiled weakly.

Next, her father pumped David's hand, then threw his arm around him, saying, "I'm real sorry about your grandmother, son. Do you know anything yet?"

David shook his head. "Not yet. Dr. Burnside's in there with her now, and we've been waiting for him to come out and talk to us."

Wylie frowned. "How long has it been?"

"Since he arrived, you mean?"

"Yes."

"About an hour and a half."

"You mean to say he hasn't come out at all?" Wylie bellowed. "There's no excuse for that!"

David started to reply, but Wylie barreled right over him. "Does he know you're out here waiting?" he demanded, his voice getting louder.

"Yes, but—"

"You're just too damned nice, David," Wylie said, cutting David off again. "Now me, I'm not, so I'm gonna go down to that nurses' station and raise a little ruckus."

Before David could protest—and Lord knows Rachel knew better than to try to stop her father—Wylie stormed down the hall and began berating the luckless nurse who happened to be manning the station at that moment.

"Go in there and tell Dr. Burnside that we want some answers out here," he ordered in his I'm-the-boss-and-won't-accept-any-excuses voice.

"I'm very sorry, sir," the nurse said, "but I have

no authority to go inside and tell Dr. Burnside anything. Why don't you have a seat with Mrs. Hanson's relatives? I'm sure Dr. Burnside will be out when he has something to report. In the meantime, if you'll just be pa—"

"Now, you listen here, young lady. I guess you don't know who I am, but I happen to be one of the biggest supporters of this hospital. In fact, the pediatric wing is named after me, and I'm tellin' you, *I want some answers* and I want 'em now!"

He thumped his fist on the counter for emphasis, and several people who were standing talking at the other end of the corridor turned around to look.

Rachel cringed. She hated it when her father threw his weight around, yet she knew Roxanne would probably have been cheering him on, so she tried to hide her embarrassment and pretend this behavior was perfectly acceptable.

"Please don't shout at me," the nurse said. "I am not hard-of-hearing."

"Maybe not," Wylie said, his face getting red, "but you do seem to have a problem following orders."

"Mr. Carlton." The nurse glared at him. "Number one, I do know who you are. Number two, I don't care how many wings you've endowed, I do not take orders from you. Number three, I am not going to tell you again. Either you stop shouting at me and go sit down quietly, or I will call security and have you forcibly evicted."

Rachel felt a tug of admiration for the nurse. Not

many people had enough nerve to stand up to her father, and especially not in public.

Because Wylie's pride wouldn't let him back down without at least a show of resistance, he sputtered for a few more minutes, then angrily charged back down the hall, where he proceeded to lambaste the nurse, the hospital, Dr. Burnside and everyone else he could think of before finally settling down on a leather chair across from Rachel. For the next ten minutes he continued to grumble and throw venomous looks in the direction of the nurse, who completely ignored him.

Thankfully, about fifteen minutes later—just as Rachel began to worry her father might cause another scene—the double doors opened, and this time Dr. Burnside strode through. Rachel's heart beat faster. She said a silent prayer that the news would be good, and reached for Virginia's hand.

David got up and walked over to meet him. Close on his heels was Rachel's father, who gave the doctor a curt greeting.

"How is she, Doctor?" David asked.

"I'm not going to soft-soap this, David," Dr. Burnside said gravely. "Your grandmother had a serious attack, and for a while there, I was afraid we were going to lose her. However, she seems to have stabilized, and I'm feeling more optimistic about her chances."

"Thank God," Virginia said.

Rachel silently echoed Virginia's sentiments.

"But don't ask me to make any predictions right

now," the doctor continued. "We'll monitor her closely for the next twenty-four to forty-eight hours and see how she does. Then, depending on how much improvement there is, we'll be better able to tell what her prognosis is."

He went on to explain in explicit medical terms exactly what had happened to Georgina Hanson and how much damage had been done to her heart.

It was, indeed, serious, Rachel thought, studying David's face as he listened, seeing how hard all this had hit him and the fear he was trying to hide. She understood. Despite what he'd said about Rachel being his family now, his grandmother was his sole remaining link to his parents and to his past. It would be very hard on him if he were to lose her.

Oh, please, God, she prayed. *Please let her survive this. I know she can't live forever, but don't take her away from David now. He can't lose her, too. Not on top of what I'm going to tell him.*

She thought about how, this morning, she'd planned to let nothing prevent her from telling him the truth tonight. But how could she go through with it? Telling him now would be too cruel. He had more than enough to deal with without adding to his burden.

She sighed wearily. There was no help for it. The truth would have to wait until his grandmother was out of the woods.

Fleetingly she thought about the September show and all the work she still had ahead of her if she was going to fulfill her promise to Phillip Blythe. And how, if she continued to be Roxanne, she would be expected to pick up the threads of Roxanne's life, too.

How was she going to do it all?

As soon as the thought formed, she felt guilty. How could she worry about the show or anything else when David's grandmother was so ill and David was so worried?

Okay, so she wouldn't worry about the show. Not now, anyway. But pretending to be Roxanne was another story. Continuing her pretense would be ten times more difficult here than it had been in Colombé. There, the only person she'd had to worry about was David. Here, in Houston, there were dozens of pitfalls and hundreds of ways she could stumble.

Well, somehow you'll have to pull it off, because you owe David this much.

"Can I see her?" David was now saying to the doctor, and Rachel forced herself to pay attention.

"Why don't you wait until later? Right now she's heavily medicated and sleeping."

David agreed, and they continued to talk for a few more minutes. Then Dr. Burnside said, "I'm going back to my office. I've left instructions for the charge nurse to call me if there's any change at all in your grandmother's condition. If not, I'll be back about eight. Will you be here then?"

"I'll be here." David's gaze met Rachel's.

"And I'll be here with him," she said.

"Sweetheart, you don't have to stay," David said later. "I know you're tired. Why don't you go home?"

It was seven o'clock, and Rachel's father had left hours ago.

"You, too, Virginia," David added, giving the older woman a sympathetic smile. "Roxanne can drop you off on her way."

Rachel started to protest, but she realized from his expression that he was worried about Virginia, who did, indeed, look exhausted. Still, she hated leaving him by himself.

"Don't worry about me," he said, correctly divining her hesitation.

"How long are you planning to stay?"

"I want to wait until Dr. Burnside gets back."

"We'll wait with you," Virginia said.

"Yes, David, that's only an hour more," Rachel said.

"Look," he said, "it's ridiculous for all of us to stay. Nothing's happening, and I doubt anything *will* happen, so there's nothing you two can do here. Go home, get some rest. You can come back in the morning."

"Well," Rachel said, torn. She wanted to call Roxanne, so it was tempting to go.

"I'll be home by eleven at the latest, I promise. And if something should happen, I'll call you. And you, too, Virginia," he added.

As much as Rachel wanted to be there with David—if only to offer moral support—after today's events she knew it was even more imperative she talk to Roxanne as soon as possible. And she certainly couldn't call her from the hospital. "All right," she finally said. "If you really don't think we should stay..."

"I really don't." He kissed her goodbye, holding her close for a long moment.

"Don't worry, David. She's going to be okay, I'm sure of it," Rachel murmured.

He gave her a grateful smile.

Forty minutes later Rachel was once more dialing the number Roxanne had given her. The same woman answered the phone, much to Rachel's relief. At least she would not have to explain anything to anyone else.

"Hello?" she said. "This is Rachel Carlton, Roxanne's sister. Is she there, please?"

"*Sí,* Señorita Carlton, your sister is here. I will call her." And Rachel heard her saying, "Roxanne, it is your sister." There was some murmuring in the background, then the woman said, "She will be with you in a moment, *señorita.*"

A few minutes later Roxanne said, "Thank you, Señora Terraza. You can hang up now." There was a distinct click, then Roxanne said, "Rachel! Thank goodness! I didn't know what to think when I kept calling and calling and you were never there. What's going on? Why didn't you call me back?"

"I'm sorry. I, uh, I couldn't. I've been away."

"Away? I didn't know you were planning to go anywhere."

"I wasn't. It, um, was kind of a spur-of-the-moment thing."

"You? Spur of the moment?" Then she laughed.

"Well, c'mon, don't keep me in suspense. What happened? From your message today, I gather Daddy must be completely furious with me."

"Um, not exactly."

"Not exactly? What does that mean? Is he or isn't he?"

It was just beginning to sink in to Rachel how difficult this whole situation was going to be to explain. "No, he's not furious with you," she said slowly.

"Really? That's a shocker. In fact, it's hard to believe, considering how he thinks the world of David."

Not to mention you, Rachel thought. "I know, but—"

"And what about David? I'm sure *he* hates my guts."

"No, David doesn't hate your guts, either."

"You mean he's okay with this, too? They *both* are?" Roxanne's voice was incredulous. "What the heck is going on?"

Rachel hesitated. *Just say it!* "The reason David doesn't hate you and Daddy isn't furious with you," she said quickly, before she could lose her nerve, "is because neither David nor Daddy knows that you ran off with Carlos."

"What? How can they *not* know?"

"Well, um, they both think—everyone thinks—it was me who ran off to Mexico."

"You! But how? Didn't you—" She broke off abruptly. "I don't understand. What exactly are you saying?"

Taking a deep breath, Rachel said, "I'm saying that I, uh, stepped in for you, you know, like we used to do when we were younger. After you left with Carlos, I put on your wedding gown and...pretended to be you."

There was a moment of stunned silence. "You can't be serious."

Rachel grimaced. "Oh, I'm serious, all right."

"You...you took my place at the *wedding?*" Her voice rose with each word.

"Yes."

"Rachel! My God, why on earth would you *do* something like that?"

Sighing, Rachel said, "I know this will be hard for you to understand, but after you left and I thought about what it would be like to go out there and, in front of all those people, tell David what had happened. I—I just couldn't do it. He...he would have been so humiliated, and I just couldn't hurt him that way."

"But to pretend to be *me!*"

"I know, it...it seems drastic...."

"Drastic! Rachel, it's...it's *crazy*. I mean, he had to know *sometime!* I mean, you didn't plan to be me *forever*, did you?"

Rachel knew she had no right to be irritated, but that was exactly how she was beginning to feel. "No, of course I didn't plan to be you forever. I didn't plan anything. I know it was probably stupid, but I just acted on instinct."

"You can say that again."

With every word, Rachel's irritation grew. After all, Roxanne was the one who had started this whole mess, not Rachel. If Roxanne had done what Rachel had advised her to do weeks before the wedding, they would not even be having this conversation. "I planned to tell David the truth after the wedding was over, in private, so he wouldn't have to be humiliated in front of all those people," she said stiffly. "I thought that between us, we could come up with some kind of face-saving story."

There was a long moment of silence. Then, in a more subdued voice, Roxanne said, "Guess I have no right to criticize you, do I?"

"No, you don't." Then, as suddenly as it had appeared, Rachel's irritation vanished. In a softer voice she said, "Let's not fight, okay? We both did impulsive things. Now we have to figure out the best way to deal with the situation."

"You're right, and I'm sorry. But—and don't get mad—I still don't understand. You say you planned to tell him right after the wedding, but obviously, if he and Daddy still think you're me, you haven't."

"No, I haven't."

"And when you said you'd been away when I called, on this spur-of-the-moment trip, you were actually...where?"

"I was in Colombé...with David."

"On *my* honeymoon?"

All of Rachel's earlier irritation returned, and with

it, a new emotion—anger. "You know, Roxanne, we need to get something straight here. You're the one who jilted David and left me to clean up the mess. So you no longer have any legitimate claim to anything that has to do with him or the wedding."

A shocked silence followed. Then Rachel heard her sister sigh heavily. "You're right, of course. I... It's just that I'm having a hard time believing all this."

"Yes, I'm sure you are. I do know how it must sound."

"So you're saying you went to Colombé and continued to pretend to be me."

"Yes."

"And...you *slept* with David?"

"Yes." Images flickered in Rachel's mind. Images that she would never forget. Images she never *wanted* to forget.

Roxanne was silent for so long, Rachel wondered if she was still there. When she finally spoke again, Rachel could tell she was trying to sound normal, but she didn't. She sounded hurt.

"But why? Why did you do it? I know what you said, but going to Colombé...that's pretty extreme. There's got to be more to this than you've told me."

Here it was, the real moment of truth.

Rachel closed her eyes. "I did it because I'm..." She swallowed. "I'm in love with David."

"What?"

"I'm in love with David," Rachel said more firmly, opening her eyes. "I've been in love with him since

I was thirteen." It felt so liberating to say it out loud, finally, the way she'd wanted to say it for years. "I love him so much, it hurts to look at him." Her voice trembled with the passion so long denied. "I feel about him exactly the same way you said you feel about Carlos. And...and after the wedding I remembered what you said, you know, when Carlos came to the church. How sometimes in life we only get this one chance, and we have to seize it. So I seized it."

The words reverberated in the air between them.

"Oh, my God," Roxanne said softly, all trace of hurt and resentment gone. Now all Rachel heard in her twin's voice was the love and caring that had always existed between them. "Rachel, if that's true, if you've loved David all this time, then...then I can't even imagine what you must have felt when we became engaged. It...it must have been hell, and you never let on, you never said a word...."

"What would have been the point?" Rachel said with resignation. "David loved you."

"Oh, Rach... Oh, God, I'm so sorry."

"It's not your fault. You couldn't help it that he fell in love with you."

"Maybe not, but I wish I'd known. I wish you'd told me."

Rachel sighed. "Look, the past is the past. What we've got to think about now is the future."

"Yes, of course," Roxanne said slowly. "You're right. The future is what counts now. So...if I'm understanding you correctly, after all this, the wedding and the honeymoon and everything, David still doesn't know you're the one he's been with?"

"No, he still doesn't know."

"And both he...and Daddy...think you ran off to Mexico to marry Carlos."

"Yes."

"What did our dear father have to say about that?"

"He wasn't very happy."

Roxanne laughed wryly. "I have a feeling that's an understatement."

Rachel remembered the cold fury in her father's eyes when she'd told him that "Rachel" had run off. "Yes, well, you know Daddy."

Another long silence followed as each of them was lost in her own thoughts.

Then Roxanne sighed again. "You know, sweetie, I do understand now why you did what you did, and I'm not criticizing you. As you so clearly pointed out, I don't have that right. But don't you think that what we've got now is a hell of a lot worse mess than what we had before?"

Rachel grimaced. "Yes."

"Back to my original question, then. When do you plan to tell David the truth? I mean, the longer you wait, the worse it'll be."

Rachel nodded, even though no one was there to see her. "I know, and I *had* planned to tell him today."

"*Had* planned?"

"Uh-huh. But now I can't."

"Why not?"

"Because something awful's happened. His grandmother had a heart attack earlier today."

"Oh, no! Oh, dear. Is she all right?"

"I hope so." Rachel then told Roxanne all about the ordeal and everything that had happened during the day. "Anyway, just as soon as she's out of danger, I'll tell him. I promise."

"And Daddy."

"No. Not this time. You'll have to tell Daddy yourself." Rachel didn't know when she'd come to this decision, but it definitely felt right to her. It was going to be bad enough when Wylie realized the part she'd played in this whole mess. She had no intention of bearing the brunt of his initial shock and anger. As it was, it wouldn't surprise her if he ending up forgiving Roxanne for what she'd done and not forgiving Rachel.

"You're right," Roxanne said after a bit. "I *should* be the one to tell Daddy. Oh, man, that's gonna be fun."

"Think about *me,*" Rachel said. "He'll probably never speak to me again."

"Aw, come on, maybe it won't be *that* bad."

"No, it'll probably be worse."

Roxanne chuckled. "We're a pair, aren't we?"

After a moment Rachel laughed, too. Better to laugh than cry, she thought.

"Just let me know when it's safe to call him," Roxanne said.

"Okay. I should know more about David's grandmother's condition in a few days. Hopefully, then I can come clean with him, and you can call Daddy."

"So you're gonna call me, right?"

"Yes. Will you be there, at this same number?"

"For the time being. Carlos expects a new assignment within the next month, so it would be foolish for us to try to find a place of our own for such a short time."

"What's it like, living there with his parents? Are they nice?"

"Oh, they're wonderful people. I was afraid they wouldn't like me. Carlos kept telling me it would be okay, but until I got here and saw that they were every bit as nice as he had said, I was worried. Anyway, they're great, and I know you'll love them, too, when you meet them. And it's no problem staying here, because their home is *enormous*. Bigger than Daddy's."

That was saying something, Rachel thought, because the Carlton family home could easily house several families.

"In fact, Carlos and I have our own separate wing. That's common in aristocratic Mexican families, you know—having these *apartamentos* for the sons in the family. I do wish I had all of my things here, though. I was going to ask you to send the rest of my clothes, but I guess you need them if you're pretending to be me." This last was said wryly.

Rachel grimaced. "I'm sorry."

"Oh, it's okay. Carlos has been buying me stuff

right and left. And I can go out and get anything I need." She lowered her voice. "The Terrazas are very rich. I had no idea. And they're very generous. Anyway, once I've talked to Daddy, maybe I'll fly home and take care of packing up my stuff and getting rid of what I don't want."

"All right."

They talked awhile longer, then Roxanne said, "Are you going to tell David you talked to me? Me as you, I mean."

"Yes, I think I'll have to. He'd wonder, otherwise."

"Well, be sure and tell him I'm pulling for his grandmother."

"I will."

"And sweetie?"

"Yes."

"I love you. You know that, don't you?"

"Yes," said Rachel, swallowing over the lump in her throat. "I know that."

It was long past midnight when David finally got home. He was sure Roxanne would be asleep. But when he walked into their bedroom she was propped up in bed, reading, and his heart lifted and some of his exhaustion fell away. She put down her book and smiled at him. "Hi."

"Hi." He walked over to the bed and leaned down to kiss her. A faint trace of something light and flowery clung to her skin, a welcome change from the smells of sickness he'd just left.

"How's your grandmother doing? Did you get to see her?" Her blue eyes were filled with sympathy and concern.

He nodded wearily. "Yeah, but only for a minute. She was groggy and I'm not sure she even realized I was there." He sat on the side of the bed and took her hand. "You know, I thought I was prepared, but it was still a shock. She looked so frail and old. I don't know. It suddenly hit me that she's not going to be around much longer."

The realization had hit him hard, and he'd had to get out of her room, away from the medicinal smells and the machines and the tubes.

"I'm sorry," Roxanne said quietly.

"I know." He squeezed her hand.

"You look tired."

"I am. I'm beat. I think I'll get ready for bed."

Quickly stripping off his clothes and tossing them in the direction of the hamper, he headed for the bathroom. When he emerged a few minutes later, she had turned off her bedside lamp. Picking his way carefully in the darkened room, he walked to his side of the bed and climbed in beside her. He groaned, feeling the tension of the day in every cramped and aching muscle.

"You okay?" she said.

Suddenly he didn't even have the strength to answer, let alone move, even though all he had been able to think of during the drive home was being with her, holding her and drawing strength from the knowledge that she loved him and would be there for him no matter what.

She caressed his cheek. And then, as if she knew exactly what he needed, she put her arms around him and cradled his head against her soft breasts. He closed his eyes, warmth and peace seeping through him. The last thing he was conscious of before falling into a deep, dreamless sleep was her soft voice whispering, "I love you, David."

Rachel held him for a long time. Her heart ached with a pain she knew would never go away. There was no justification for what she had done to David. She could tell herself she had simply seized her chance for happiness, but what she'd really done had been monumentally selfish.

She had taken what she'd wanted at his expense.

She could see that clearly now.

In this past week they had forged a bond, and he had come to depend on her. Now, when he found out the truth, he was going to be hurt so much more than he would've been hurt by Roxanne's initial defection.

And somehow, in the lonely years ahead, she would have to learn to live with that.

Chapter Ten

Rachel kept David company most of the following day. She tried not to think about the work she was neglecting and the possible career disaster she was courting. She tried not to think about what Phillip Blythe would say or do if she didn't fulfill her promise to him.

She wondered if she should call him, tell him that there'd been a family crisis, and she would have to wait until next year for the promised show.

That was probably the sensible thing to do, but the thought of doing it was depressing. Phillip Blythe might change his mind about her and her work if she canceled the show now. Maybe he was the kind of person who believed art should come first and that a true artist would continue to work no matter what else was going on in his life.

I can't lose this opportunity. Not on top of losing David. Somehow, after this time with David is over, the work will get done, even if I have to work twenty-four hours a day.

So she did nothing about Phillip Blythe and the impending show. Instead, she sat with David and gave him what moral support she could.

It turned out to be an encouraging day, because his grandmother showed steady improvement. David visited her several times and, a little after five o'clock that afternoon, Rachel was told she could go in with him during the next visiting period.

Although David had told her what to expect, she was still shocked to see the changes wrought by Georgina's heart attack. Oh, God, she was so pale. She looked ten years older than the last time Rachel had seen her. With a heavy heart, Rachel forced a smile to her lips and tried hard not to show how dismayed she was by the older woman's altered appearance.

"Hello, Mrs. Hanson," she said brightly. "You certainly gave us a scare." She leaned over to kiss the older woman's cheek. Its papery thinness was another reminder of Georgina's age and frailty.

Georgina gave her a weak smile. "I'm sorry you didn't have a better homecoming, my dear." Even her voice sounded older, with a threadiness that hadn't been there before.

"Now, Gran, don't you worry about that," David

said, taking his grandmother's hand. "All we care about is that you get better."

"I'm trying," she whispered.

They didn't stay long. It was obvious it took too much effort for David's grandmother to carry on a conversation, so after a few more soothing remarks about how well she was doing, they left.

"Oh, David, she looks so frail," Rachel said as they walked out of the CCU.

He nodded sadly. "I know."

Rachel was immediately sorry for what she'd said, and would have given anything if she could have taken her words back. What a nitwit she was! Why hadn't she said something to ease the strain he was under instead of pointing out things better left unsaid?

She put her arm around his waist. "But she'll get stronger. She's a fighter."

"That's what I keep telling myself."

At six o'clock David tried to persuade Rachel to go home, but she insisted on staying and having dinner with him. There was no way she could go to the town house and paint, not tonight, and that was the only thing she cared about doing other than being with David.

They headed for the cafeteria, because he hated to be too far away from the hospital, just in case things should take a turn for the worse.

"I've been so worried about my grandmother, I haven't even asked you about Rachel," David said once they'd gotten their food and found a table. "Did you talk to her yesterday?"

"Yes," Rachel said, ignoring the twinge of guilt she always felt when they discussed this subject. "She sent her love and asked me to tell you she was praying for your grandmother."

"Those two always got along well." He took a bite of mashed potatoes.

"Yes," Rachel said. "I—I know she loves your grandmother. Very much." She reached for the pepper and shook some onto her salad.

He smiled. "You want to know something funny? I think my grandmother always secretly hoped Rachel and I would get together."

Rachel was so startled, she nearly spilled her water.

"Oh, not that she doesn't like *you,*" he hastened to add, "because she does. It's just that she always thought Rachel and I were more alike." He began to butter his roll.

Before Rachel could think how to answer this unexpected disclosure, he gave her a teasing smile. "But if she could have seen us on our honeymoon, she would've known how compatible we *really* are."

Rachel could feel herself blushing.

David laughed. "I never guessed you'd be the kind to get embarrassed."

"I don't usually," Rachel said. She could have kicked herself. She was doing a terrible job of being Roxanne.

"Hey, I *like* it." David reached under the table and

stroked her knee. His voice fell. "I like everything about my wife."

Rachel swallowed. "David," she said weakly.

His smile was slow and tender. "I know. Not the time or the place." Removing his hand, he said briskly. "Well? Were we right? Are Rachel and Carlos married?"

Rachel nodded, relieved at the change in subject. She told him everything Roxanne had said. "She seems really happy, David. And contented. More so than I've ever seen her before." This was better. Now she was telling him the truth. Well, she corrected herself, *almost* the truth.

"Good. I'm glad. Rachel deserves to be happy. How about your father? Did you tell him you'd talked to her?"

"No, not yet."

He cut a piece of his chicken fried steak and lifted it to his mouth. "Why not?"

"I really haven't had a chance," she hedged.

He gave her a thoughtful look. "Yeah, well, I don't blame you for putting it off. It won't be pleasant."

After that, he dropped this subject, too, and Rachel was thankful. Even though, in her mind, she substituted Roxanne's name for hers, it was still very difficult to talk to him about any of this. She was constantly afraid of saying something she shouldn't.

For a while they silently ate their dinner. When they were almost finished, he said, "Did Rachel say anything about coming home?"

"No. She said they're waiting to see where Carlos's next assignment would be. I imagine they won't make any plans until they know where they'll be living and when he has to report."

David nodded. "Did she have any idea where he might go next?"

"I don't think so. She didn't say."

"Maybe they'll have time to come to Houston in between."

"Maybe." Rachel guessed this would depend on how her father took the news of which twin had *really* gone to Mexico.

"If they don't," David mused, "maybe we could visit them. I still have vacation time coming and, technically, I should use it before the end of the year."

"We'll see," Rachel said noncommittally.

"'Cause I'd like to meet him, make sure he's good enough for her."

Rachel could hardly meet his eyes.

"Of course, we can't make any plans until we know how Gran's gonna do."

Rachel nodded. She fervently hoped David's grandmother got better soon, not only because she loved the older woman, but because she wasn't sure how much longer she could keep this pretense going. Lying to people you loved was too hard, and she was feeling worse and worse about it with each passing day.

On Thursday morning, three days after Georgina's heart attack, Dr. Burnside announced that David's grandmother was out of the woods. "For now, anyway," he cautioned. But then he smiled. "I'm optimistic, though. She's a fighter, and that's half the battle."

"How much longer will she have to stay in the CCU?" David asked.

Rachel knew leaving the CCU was the true test of whether or not her doctors considered David's grandmother to be out of danger.

"We're moving her to a private room later today."

Rachel and David grinned at each other.

"I think this calls for a celebration," David said once the doctor had gone.

Rachel agreed, so they went to his favorite Mexican restaurant for lunch.

"I don't know what I would have done without you the past few days," he said after their waitress had taken their order and served them a basket of warm chips and a bowl of salsa.

The expression in his eyes, so filled with love, pierced Rachel's heart.

"I kept thinking, even if the worst should happen, I wouldn't be alone, I'd have you."

Oh, David... "I—I'm glad I could help."

His smile made her want to cry.

"Have I told you lately how much I love you, Mrs. Hanson?" he said softly.

Rachel was too choked up to reply. She hurriedly excused herself, saying she needed to go to the ladies' room. David's expression was tender and indulgent.

She knew he thought she was simply embarrassed by his comments instead of devastated by the knowledge that he felt safe opening his soul to her and that she was betraying him in a way no one should ever be betrayed.

How was it she had never thought about how he would feel while she was seizing the day? Her only hesitation had been that there would be consequences to her act, but she'd never once thought that she wouldn't be the only one paying them. In her zeal to protect David from humiliation at Roxanne's hands, she, Rachel, had done something far worse.

It was with a heavy heart that she finally rejoined him at the table. And throughout the rest of the meal, no matter how she tried not to, she couldn't stop thinking about what he'd said and how he'd said it, and she knew, if she lived to be one hundred, she would never forgive herself for the pain she was going to cause him.

When they returned to the hospital, Georgina was just getting settled into her room. A little while later they were told they could go in.

This time, Rachel felt encouraged by the way David's grandmother looked. Her color was back, and she was propped up in bed and wearing a pretty pink robe.

"Hey, Granny, you're looking better," David said, a teasing twinkle in his eye.

"Virginia brought me some of my own clothes," Georgina said. "But I wish I could do something about this hair. It hasn't been fixed in days, and it looks terrible. I know I'm going to be getting a lot of visitors, and I don't want them to see me looking like this."

Rachel figured Georgina was right, if the amount of flowers and cards that had been sent were any indication. "Do you want me to see what I can do with your hair?" she offered.

Georgina's eyes lit up. "Yes, please, my dear. And maybe you could help me put on some makeup, too."

"You *must* be feeling better," David said, laughing, "if you're ready for primping. Tell you what. I'll let you two girls do your thing, and I'll go outside. Call me when you're done."

So Rachel proceeded to do what she could to make Georgina look better. While she worked on her hair and makeup, Georgina watched her out of those eyes that were so eerily like David's.

"I guess I don't have to ask if you're happy," Georgina said. "I can see how you feel about David every time you look at him."

Rachel composed herself before meeting the older woman's gaze. "Yes, I'm happy," she said softly. "David is a wonderful man."

Georgina nodded. "Yes, he is." She smiled. "And I'd say that even if he weren't my grandson."

Rachel smiled, too. "Of course you would. After all, you're not prejudiced."

"Not in the least." She looked at herself in the

mirror Rachel held up. "By the way, have you talked with, um, Rachel since you got home?"

Was that a slight hesitation before she'd said "Rachel"? Or was Rachel feeling so guilty she was seeing and hearing things that weren't there at all? "Yes. I've spoken to her twice. She's been worried about you, and called yesterday to find out how you were doing."

"And how is *she* doing?"

"She's doing just fine. She and Carlos were married last week, and she seems very much in love."

Georgina nodded thoughtfully.

Rachel looked away. David's grandmother was far too astute, and there was something about the speculative look in her eyes that disturbed Rachel. Could she possibly suspect something? No. How could she? It was just Rachel's guilty conscience at work.

"And your father?" Georgina said. "Has he talked with her yet?"

"No, not yet."

"Is he still angry?"

"I'm sure he is."

Georgina chuckled. "I certainly would like to be a little mouse and hear *that* conversation. Bet it'll burn up the wires between here and Mexico."

Rachel made a noncommittal sound. She had no such desire, because she knew once her father and Roxanne *did* talk, her charade would be over.

And that conversation would take place very soon, because now that David's grandmother was so much better Rachel could no longer avoid the inevitable.

It was time to tell David the truth.

The word spread fast.

By three o'clock Georgina had several visitors and two more bouquets of flowers.

"Place smells like a mortuary," she said, but Rachel could tell she was pleased by the attention.

David grinned. In an aside to Rachel, he said, "I think we can leave, don't you?"

Rachel nodded gratefully. She was worn out with pretending to be Roxanne to all these newcomers.

They kissed Georgina goodbye, promised to come back in the morning and made their escape.

"I should go into the office," David said, pressing the button for the elevator. "When I talked to Carole earlier, she said the place was in chaos."

"Something go wrong with the move?"

"No, they got moved okay. It's just another ordinary, everyday crisis."

Rachel heard the note of weariness, and guilt attacked her afresh. She'd been so consumed with her own problems, she had forgotten that David had problems of his own. *And you're going to be adding to them.* "If you need to go in, go," she said hurriedly, trying not to think about what lay ahead of her. "I have things I should do, too."

"You sure you don't mind?"

"No. Of course not."

The elevator pinged and the doors slid open.

"I'll try to get home early," he said as they walked inside.

"Okay."

When they reached the ground floor, they walked outside together. Halfway across the crosswalk that connected the hospital to the parking area, they met Rachel's father. He had a large, gift-wrapped box in his hand.

"You're not leaving?" he said to Rachel, his disappointment obvious.

"I was planning to. I've been here since early this morning, and David's grandmother has other visitors now."

Wylie nodded. "Come have a cup of coffee with me first. I've hardly seen you since you got back."

Rachel didn't want to. But how could she refuse? Roxanne wouldn't have.

"All right," she said reluctantly.

After saying goodbye to David, she and her father headed for the cafeteria.

Once they were settled with their coffee, he said bluntly, "Have you talked to your sister?"

Rachel's heart gave a painful lurch. "Y-yes," she stammered. She was immediately furious with herself. Why was it her father always had this effect on her?

"When?"

"I, um, talked to her Monday night and again yesterday."

Her father's mouth tightened. "Where is she?"

"At the home of Carlos's parents in Veracruz."

Wylie stirred his coffee, and it was a few moments before he spoke again. "Are they married?"

"Yes."

He pondered this disclosure for another long moment. Finally he looked up. "Why hasn't she called me?"

Rachel shrugged, picking her words carefully. She wanted to be as truthful as possible. "Maybe she's been afraid to call you."

"That's typical," he said bitterly. "She's just like your mother. Scared of her own shadow."

"That's not fair, Daddy. And...and it really bothers me to hear you talk like that."

Rachel was as surprised as he looked. Even Roxanne rarely contradicted their father.

"Mother was a wonderful person, gentle and kind," she continued, "and completely unselfish. People loved her. *I* loved her."

"I loved her, too," her father retorted, obviously stung.

"Well, then, don't say things like that."

"I didn't mean anything by it," he mumbled.

"Maybe not, but it's hurtful anyway." It was amazing, but Rachel was feeling better by the minute. These were things she'd wanted to say for years. "You're right that mother didn't like confrontations. And Rachel doesn't, either. But that doesn't mean either one of them was or is a coward."

"Well," Wylie grumbled, "it sure as hell was cowardly of your sister to run off without telling me."

"Maybe she felt she didn't have a choice."

"That's bull."

"It's not bull. We all know how you lose your temper when you're crossed," Rachel noted. "Maybe she didn't want to ruin the wedding with a big blowup."

"Well, as far as I'm concerned, she ruined it anyway. Her running off like that was all anyone could talk about at the reception."

"Is *that* all you care about? What people are saying about us?"

Wylie looked down at his coffee and avoided her eyes. "No." When he finally looked up, his expression was bleak. "Do you think Rachel's *ever* going to call me?"

The hurt in his eyes shocked Rachel. Could he possibly care more than she'd imagined?

"She'll call you," she said softly. "She's probably just giving you time to cool down."

"Cool down, huh? I ought to tan her hide a good one," he said, returning to his normal bluster. Then his voice softened, too. "I just want to talk to her. Make sure she's all right and that this Carlos is good enough for her."

"She's more than all right," Rachel assured him. "She's very happy. And Carlos is a good man, Daddy. He's bright and ambitious and he comes from a very good family. And despite what I know you thought, he didn't marry her for your money. His family is wealthy." She told him some of what Roxanne had said.

Her father looked as if he'd like to dispute what she'd said, but he didn't. "Is she plannin' to come home before his next assignment?" he asked when she'd finished.

Rachel smiled. "I imagine that's going to depend on you…and how you act when she *does* call you."

They talked a while longer, then her father said, "Why don't you give me Rachel's phone number? Maybe I'll call her."

Rachel's heart gave a painful bump. "I, um, don't have it here."

"Well, how about callin' me at the office tomorrow and giving it to me then?"

Since Rachel could do nothing else, she said she would.

He smiled and wadded up his empty paper cup. "Well, guess I'd better go up and see Georgina now, because I have a dinner meeting at six."

They both stood and hugged goodbye, and Rachel sadly wondered if this might be the last time she would ever hug her father, because despite today's revelation about his feelings for her, she wasn't sure how he would handle what had *really* happened.

Rather than go home to David's house, after leaving the hospital Rachel headed for her town house. She still hadn't signed the contract with Blythe Gallery, and she needed to do that immediately. In fact, she could drop it off at the gallery on her way to David's.

She also needed to call Roxanne, and she preferred to do it from the town house.

"Thank God you're home," she said when Roxanne answered her call an hour later. "I've got a lot to tell you. First of all, David's grandmother seems to have passed the crisis."

"Oh, that's wonderful."

"Yes. And because she has, I'm planning to tell David the truth tonight."

"Good. I've been so worried about this."

"I know. Me, too."

"I guess that means I can call Daddy tomorrow."

"Uh-huh. In fact, it would be best if you'd call him first thing, because he's asked me to give him your number so he can call you himself." Rachel grimaced. "Of course, he has no idea who he'd really be calling."

"I can't call him first thing. Carlos and I are leaving at seven for Mexico City, so it'll have to wait until we get home tomorrow afternoon. We should be back about six, though."

Rachel chewed on her lower lip and tried to think what to do.

"Why don't you tell him I'm going to be away and said I'd call him tomorrow night?" Roxanne suggested.

"I guess that would work."

"So Daddy knows we've talked."

"Yes. He asked me, so I told him the truth."

"What did he say?"

"It was a funny thing. He didn't seem nearly as mad as he had before. In fact, he said he wished you'd call him. Of course, he still thinks you're me. Oh, God. This is so complicated. Anyway, I assured him that Carlos was a really great guy and he didn't marry you for your money."

"Is that what he thought?"

"You know Daddy."

"Yes," Roxanne said wryly. "I do." They were silent for a few moments, then she said, "Good luck tonight, sweetie. I know this is going to be much harder for you than it will be for me."

"Thanks," Rachel said.

After they hung up, Rachel sat there thinking about what she would say to David. How she would say it. Even the thought of the upcoming confrontation made her heart beat faster and her throat go dry.

He was going to be so angry.

And so hurt.

She hugged herself.

What would he do? Would he order her out of the house tonight? Tell her he never wanted to see her again? She felt sick to her stomach as she imagined how he would despise her afterward.

Oh, David, my darling, I'm so sorry.

She looked at her watch. Four o'clock. David had said he'd try to get home early. By six, he should be there. So it was only a matter of a couple of hours before the moment of truth.

Please, God, help me.

Fighting tears, she picked up the Blythe Gallery contract. She tried to read through it again, but she couldn't concentrate. Finally she just signed it. What did it matter if it wasn't worded exactly right or if she might be able to get better terms by negotiating with Phillip Blythe? What did anything matter next to the loss of the only man she would ever love?

Chapter Eleven

An hour later, calm again, Rachel decided she might as well try to look her best for the coming ordeal, so she showered and washed her hair. She also took special care with her makeup and clothes, putting on a silky blue pants outfit with a long tunic top from Roxanne's trousseau that David had said he liked.

She wondered if she should cook dinner. Wouldn't it be more considerate to wait and tell David everything after dinner instead of upsetting him before he'd had a chance to eat? Yes, of course it would be.

She hoped there would be something in the house she could fix. After rummaging through the freezer, she decided that by using the defrost feature on the microwave, she could quick-thaw a couple of the frozen chicken breasts she'd found. And she discovered a box of brown and wild rice in the pantry. The vegetable keeper yielded a tomato and half a cucumber, so she could make a salad, too.

So far, so good.

Bread was a problem, though, but there was enough time to make a fast trip to the bakery at the corner and pick up a loaf of freshly baked olive bread, one of their specialties. And while she was there, she would buy one of their amaretto cheesecakes, too.

Why not? she thought wryly. *The dying man deserves a hearty last meal.*

Although which one of them—she or David—qualified as the dying man was a debatable question.

At six-thirty everything was ready. The chicken breasts were marinating in a concoction of soy sauce, lemon juice and herbs, ready for broiling as soon as David walked in the door. The rice was cooked and in a serving dish—all she'd have to do was nuke it when they were ready to eat. The salad was made and, along with the cheesecake, waited in the refrigerator. The bread, ready for slicing, sat on the cutting board. Wine was chilling in the ice bucket. The table was set, candles ready to be lighted, and Rachel had even bought a bunch of flowers at the open-air flower market in Rice Village.

A perfect setting for murder, she thought, wryly amused by her newly discovered penchant for melodrama.

It is *murder! You'll be murdering every vestige of friendship and respect David ever had for you.*

Grimly she pushed the negative thought from her mind and focused on her preparations. Somehow, it seemed very important that everything around her look perfect. So she walked around the house plumping pillows, straightening pictures, sorting through David's CDs until she found one she liked, picking imaginary lint off the furniture—anything and everything to keep from thinking.

But finally she could find nothing else to do. She looked around desperately. She knew she had to keep busy if she wanted to stay calm. She tried reading the paper, but couldn't concentrate. She turned off the CD player and turned on the TV set, but she couldn't sit still.

Turning off the set, she paced back and forth, looking out the front window every few minutes.

Where was he?

Every time she heard a car, her heart lurched. She was terrified, and yet, perversely, now that she knew she could no longer put off telling David the truth, she wanted to get it over with quickly. This waiting was excruciating.

She stared at the empty street.

Come on, David. Come on.

At seven he still hadn't come home. By now Rachel had worn a path in the carpet, and her stomach felt as if it had been taken over by aliens. If he didn't come home soon, she might have a nervous breakdown.

At seven-fifteen the phone rang.

Rachel raced to answer it.

"Sweetheart," David said, "I'm sorry, I know I said I'd be home early, but we've got another crisis here. This time it's on one of the rigs, and I can't leave." He sounded exhausted.

"It's okay, David. Don't worry about it." It wasn't okay, but what else could she say? She could tell he felt bad. She certainly didn't want to add to his problems.

Oh, that's funny. You don't want to add *to his problems? Like telling him he's not really married isn't going to upset him?*

"I'll call you when I have a better idea of how long I'll be," he continued wearily.

They said goodbye and Rachel slowly replaced the receiver in its cradle. She leaned against the kitchen counter and closed her eyes. Why tonight, of all nights, did David have to be detained? She wondered if some mischievous force in the universe was at work. A force that wanted to make her suffer as much as possible.

At eight o'clock David called again. "It's gonna be another hour at least. Why don't you go ahead and eat without me?"

"No, David, I'll wait for you to get here. I don't mind." She wasn't the least bit hungry. This meal had been for him, not her.

Once more she tried to find something to occupy her mind. She thought about her sketchbook. If only she had it here. But she'd been afraid to bring it to David's house, afraid that even if she hid it, somehow he might see it. She eyed the notepad sitting next to the telephone. That would do.

For the next two hours she sketched remembered scenes from Colombé, losing herself in the work and recapturing her feelings of well-being and happiness. By ten o'clock—with no further word from David—she had sketches for almost a dozen possible new paintings. One in particular really excited her. It was a sketch of a street scene from the main bazaar in Colombé. Rachel had taken a whole roll of film that day, and now she wished she'd gotten the film developed, but in the confusion and turmoil of Georgina's heart attack, she had completely forgotten about it.

Well, she thought, she could do that tomorrow.

At ten o'clock she tore the sketches from the notepad and stuffed them deep into her purse. She didn't want David seeing them before she'd had a chance to talk to him. That is, if he ever got home.

Walking to the front window, she peered down the street. Several cars drove by, but none was David's.

Now that she was no longer busy sketching, her stomach began its nervous fluttering once again. If David didn't come home soon, she wasn't sure she would be able to stand it.

Finally, at ten-thirty, David walked in the door. All Rachel had to do was take one look at him to see how completely worn out he was.

"I'm sorry about dinner," he said, putting his arms around her and hugging her.

"It doesn't matter." She gently extricated herself from his embrace, avoiding his eyes and busying herself by walking to the wet bar and pouring him a glass of wine. She handed it to him. "Do you feel like eating now, or should I put the food away?"

He sank onto the couch and closed his eyes. "I'm too tired to eat. Do you mind?"

"Of course not."

He opened his eyes and smiled up at her. "I'm really sorry, sweetheart. I know you went to a lot of trouble getting it all ready."

"Don't worry about that. That's not important."

He closed his eyes again, laying his head back. "Today was a bitch of a day."

Rachel wanted to put her arms around him. Kiss him and soothe him. Make the worries of the day fade away. But she didn't have the right to do that. It would just make her job harder. Besides, to continue to deceive him was cruel. But how could she tell him when he was so tired?

Quit stalling and looking for reasons to put off the inevitable!

Rachel swallowed. Clasping her hands together to still their trembling, she said softly, "David..."

"Hmm?" He didn't open his eyes.

Her heart wrenched. She had never seen him look so worn-out.

While she hesitated, he opened his eyes again and

took a drink of his wine. He sighed heavily. "I really hate my job. I could walk away from there tomorrow and never miss it."

Rachel could think of nothing worse than hating your job. Well, she could think of one thing worse—David hating her—but that was beside the point. "Why do stay there, then?"

"You know why."

"David, if you were to leave, your grandmother might be disappointed for a while, but she'd get over it. If I were you, I'd tell her how I feel. She loves you, and if you explained your idea about that boys' ranch, I think she'd be proud of you."

At her words, David frowned, and for a moment Rachel wondered if she'd said something she shouldn't have.

"That's easy for you to say," he said. "You're not the one she's counting on."

She stiffened, oddly hurt by his reaction. "I'm sorry. You're right. It's none of my business."

"That's not what I meant."

But she knew it *was* what he'd meant. That frown had spoken volumes.

"Sweetheart..." He put his wineglass down, then reached up, drawing her down onto his lap. Rachel knew it was a mistake to let him, but couldn't summon up enough willpower to resist.

"C'mon," he said softly. "I didn't mean to hurt your feelings." He caressed her cheek, rubbing his thumb back and forth and smiling down into her eyes.

"Anything that concerns me, concerns you. I'm just tired." He lowered his head to kiss her.

Rachel knew she should pull away. If she let him kiss her, her resolve would weaken, and she *had* to tell him tonight. But even as she told herself this, her eyelids drifted shut and she lifted her face.

Tunneling his hands through her hair, he kissed her deeply and hungrily.

"David," she said as one kiss became two, two became three.

"Let's go to bed," he said, his voice rough with desire. He stroked her breast.

"David, wait. I— There's something I have to talk to you about." She tried to pull away, she really did, but he held her fast.

"Later," he muttered, kissing her again, letting his mouth trail from her lips to her throat.

Rachel closed her eyes. They hadn't made love in days, and her body cried out for his touch. Still, some semblance of reason remained. "Please, David, there's something I have to tell you."

He stood, lifting her up with him. "Whatever it is, it can wait."

"No, David, really—"

He silenced her by kissing her again. Then he carried her into the bedroom. "I've been thinking about this all day." Slowly he set her on her feet.

Pressing her close, his hands cupped her bottom, and she could feel how much he wanted her.

All Rachel's good intentions evaporated.

She loved him so much.

And this would be the last time she'd be with him like this. The very last time.

What harm could one more night do?

So she lifted her arms and twined them around his neck. And within moments she was lost in the rosy world where she and David were the only people who existed.

"We find the defendant guilty as charged," said the jury foreman.

"Poll the jurors," said the judge, a dark, forbidding man with accusing eyes.

Rachel trembled as, one by one, the jurors stood.

"Guilty!" said the first juror.

"Guilty!" said the second juror.

"Guilty!" said the third juror.

Each looked at her as if she were lower than a snake. But she didn't blame them. She was *lower than a snake.*

When the twelfth juror had made her pronouncement, David walked to the front of the courtroom. He faced her, his beloved face filled with contempt.

"It's up to you, Mr. Hanson," said the judge. "Shall we show her mercy?"

"She deserves no mercy," David said.

"No mercy!" snarled the prosecutor.

"No mercy!" shouted the jury.

"No mercy!" yelled the spectators.

"Put her in the dungeon and throw away the key," David continued coldly.

"David," Rachel pleaded, "I love you. I never meant to hurt you."

"You don't know the meaning of the word love," David said. His eyes were flat as they met hers. "I never want to see you again." And then he walked away, out of the courtroom and out of Rachel's life. She reached toward him, but he didn't turn around.

Rachel jerked awake. She was sweating, and her heart was pounding like a piston. The dream had been so vivid. For a brief moment she felt as if it had really happened.

But no.

There was David, sleeping soundly beside her, still blissfully unaware that in just a few hours she was going to blast his world to pieces.

Rachel shivered, the memory of the way he'd looked at her in the dream a chilling reminder that even though no one was going to put her in jail for what she'd done, if she was banished from David's life, she would be in a different kind of prison.

Her heart ached with a deep hopelessness as she watched him sleep. *Oh, David, David, I love you so much. I'd give anything in the world to change things.* How had she ever imagined she was doing the right thing? What demon had possessed her?

Turning her pillow over, she tried to get comfortable. Tried to go back to sleep. But her troubled thoughts would not let her rest. On and on they tumbled, a relentless barrage of accusations that pummeled her mercilessly. By the time she finally did fall into an exhausted slumber, it was close to dawn.

The next thing she knew, David was jumping out of bed.

"Wh-what's wrong?" she said, rubbing her eyes. The bedroom was bright, even though the blinds were closed.

"Dammit!" he said through clenched teeth. "I overslept again. And I've got a meeting at eight." He disappeared into the bathroom, and seconds later she heard the shower.

She looked at the bedside clock. It read 7:30. Running her hands through her hair, she tried to gather her fuzzy thoughts.

And then, with perfect clarity, she remembered everything. Last night. How she'd planned everything, and how her plans had been foiled by David's late homecoming. She remembered how she'd tried to talk to him, but how he'd broken down her resistance by making love to her.

Oh, dear God, I can't wait any longer. I have to tell him this morning. Because even if I wanted to put if off again, I couldn't. Roxanne is calling Daddy today!

Scrambling out of bed, Rachel threw on her bathrobe and hurried out to the kitchen. After putting the coffee on, she downed two aspirin, then used the guest bathroom to wash her face, comb her hair and brush her teeth.

Afterward, she felt marginally better, and she sat at the kitchen table and waited for the coffee to finish brewing and David to emerge from the bathroom.

A few minutes later she heard him moving around in the bedroom. Soon he would come out to the kitchen. Knowing David, he would probably be planning to take his coffee in the car and drink it on the way.

No matter what he says, you have to tell him before he leaves for the office.

Her stomach felt hollow, and she pressed her hands tightly against it. Oh, God. She should have told him last night. This was terrible, telling him this morning when he was late and would be stressed out about missing his meeting and whatever else awaited him at the office.

In the bedroom, a drawer slammed.

Rachel's heart skidded.

She began to pray.

Even though he was going to be late for the meeting with Mark Taylor from Taylor Security Systems, David wasn't sorry about last night.

Remembering, he smiled.

Roxanne.

He loved her so much. Even more than he'd loved her before. *Much* more than he'd loved her before, he corrected.

These past two weeks with her had been the best weeks of his life. Even the scare about his grandmother hadn't diminished his happiness and contentment with his marriage.

Roxanne was so perfect, he thought as he struggled to get his tie just right. Quiet when he needed quiet, fun when he needed fun, and loving when he needed love.

Sexy, too.

He grinned. Well, that went without saying. Finishing with his tie, he grabbed his suit jacket and briefcase and headed for the kitchen. The smell of freshly brewed coffee greeted him. Roxanne, who had been sitting at the kitchen table, stood.

"David..."

He walked over to her and kissed her. "I'm sorry, sweetheart, but I haven't got time for breakfast this morning."

"I know, but David, I need to—"

"You don't need to do anything. I just want a cup of coffee in one of those insulated things, okay?" As he was talking, he walked to the cupboard and took out the insulated mug.

"David, please, I *have* to talk to you."

Filled mug in hand, he turned. Seeing how troubled she looked gave him a start. "What's wrong? Are you sick?"

"No, but I—"

"Good. For a minute there, you had me wor—"

His words were cut off by the peal of the telephone. Swearing under his breath, he reached for the portable phone on the kitchen counter. "Hello."

"Hello, David?" said a female voice.

"Yes?"

"What're you doing home? Shouldn't you be out earning a living?"

David grinned, finally recognizing Paula's bantering tone. "It's Paula," he mouthed.

Roxanne frowned and waved her hands in a "no" gesture.

"We slept in," he said. "I was just on my way out the door."

"Well, guess I'll have to settle for talking to Roxanne, then," Paula said, laughing.

"Okay. Here she is." He shrugged in apology. He didn't have time to fend off Paula. Dropping a kiss on Roxanne's forehead, he handed her the phone, saying, "We'll talk tonight, I promise."

Then he waved goodbye and left.

Rachel felt like crying as she reluctantly accepted the phone. Taking a few seconds to compose herself, she waited before saying, "Hello?"

"Hey, how's the old married woman doing?"

"Fine."

"Fine? Just *fine?* Come on, I'm your best friend. I want to hear all about it. How was the honeymoon? Wonderful? Fabulous? Or just great?"

From somewhere, a strength Rachel hadn't known she possessed kicked in and she was able to make her tone light and bantering, just the way Roxanne would have. "I'll never tell."

There was a knowing chuckle from Paula's end.

"That means it was fabulous." She sighed. "Too bad those honeymoon feelings don't last."

"Speak for yourself."

Paula laughed again. "Just wait, that's what I thought, too, when old married people told me the same thing. Trust me, that state of I-can't-get-enough-of-him doesn't last long. I give it three months, tops. Then you'll be looking for excuses not to do it, just like the rest of us."

They continued in this vein for another ten minutes or so, with Paula teasing and Rachel doing her best to return her quips with quips of her own. Then Paula's voice turned serious. "I was going to holler at you for not calling me as soon as you got home, but then I heard about David's grandmother and realized you were probably spending all your time at the hospital."

"Yes," Rachel said, relieved to get past the topic of sex.

"How's she doing?"

"She's doing great. She's in a private room now." Rachel went on to describe Georgina Hanson's condition and what her doctors had said.

"So when're you going back to work?" Paula said when they'd exhausted the topic of David's grandmother.

For one second Rachel almost said something about the sketches she'd finished the night before, but she caught herself in time. Paula wasn't asking about her, she was asking about Roxanne. "I, um, don't have anything scheduled until after the Fourth."

"Lucky you." Paula worked as a paralegal in the labor relations department for one of Houston's biggest oil companies and, according to Roxanne, she was always complaining about her job. "I *wish* I worked for myself and could take time off like you do."

Rachel made a noncommittal sound. She knew, again from things Roxanne had said, that even though Paula and Roxanne were close friends, Paula was envious of Roxanne. And the envy wasn't about Roxanne's job or her self-employed status so much as it was about the twins' moneyed background. Paula came from a working-class family and had always had to rely on herself alone. Yet there were things about her background that Rachel envied. Like the fact that Paula's mother was alive and healthy and that Paula and her father had a close relationship.

"Oh, I know, I shouldn't complain," Paula said, obviously not taking any offense at Rachel's silence. "I have a good job and so does Craig."

"Yes, you do." Rachel searched for a reason to terminate the conversation. She *had* to get off the phone, because it was imperative she try to get in touch with Roxanne and once again delay her impending phone call to their father.

But before she could come up with an excuse to hang up, Paula said, "Have you talked to Rachel since you got back?"

"Yes."

"Oh, good! Is she married?"

"Yes, she's married."

“Ooh, what did your father have to say about that?”

“He wasn’t real happy. But listen, Paula, I really don’t have time to tell you all about it now. I’m sorry, but I’ve got to go. I have an appointment to get my nails done, and I’m going to be late if I don’t hurry.”

“Oh, okay. But I can’t wait to hear all the poop. How about meeting me for lunch today? We could go to Treebeard’s.”

Rachel injected as much regret into her voice as she could. “Gee, I’m sorry, I’d love to, but I can’t. I already have lunch plans.”

“How about tomorrow?”

“Tomorrow’s Saturday, Paula.”

“Oh, yeah. I guess you’ve got plans. I know! Why don’t you and David have dinner with Craig and me tomorrow night?”

“I’m sorry. I don’t think we can. Not this weekend. Um, why don’t you call me Monday morning?” By then Rachel would be long gone and Roxanne would have called Paula to explain everything.

“Well, if you’re sure you can’t—”

“I’m sure. I’ll talk to you Monday. And thanks for calling. Bye.” Rachel hung up before Paula could protest further.

As soon as she heard the tone, Rachel dialed the now-familiar number in Mexico. This time another female voice answered, and Rachel had to resort to her rusty Spanish to ask for Señora Terraza. She breathed a sigh of relief when Carlos’s mother came on the line.

"I am sorry, Señorita Carlton, but my son and your sister have gone to Mexico City today," Señora Terraza said.

"Yes, I know, but I have to reach my sister. It's very important. I was hoping you'd have a number there that I might try."

"No, I'm sorry, I don't. They were going in to talk with Carlos's superiors at the foreign service office. I suppose I could try to get the number for you, if you really need it."

"No, no, that's all right." No way did Rachel want to try to track Carlos down, especially since she wasn't sure she could make herself understood if she had to talk with someone who didn't speak English. "Um, I'd just like to leave a message, though."

"Certainly."

"Please tell my sister that something prevented me from talking to David today, so she should not call our father today. That's very important. She should not call our father today."

Señora Terraza repeated Rachel's words, and Rachel could hear the question the older woman was too polite to ask. She probably thought both Rachel and Roxanne were crazy, seeing as how this was the second time Rachel had left a similar message.

"She'll understand," Rachel said.

"Do not worry. As soon as they arrive home, I will give your sister the message."

After thanking Carlos's mother, Rachel slowly hung up. She was afraid to feel relief. There was always the chance Roxanne wouldn't get the message in time. What if, for some reason, she decided to call their father from Mexico City?

Rachel knew it would be courting disaster to assume she was safe until David got home tonight. She just couldn't ignore the chance that Wylie might hear from Roxanne before Rachel could explain things to David.

Oh, God, that would be horrible.

She bit on her bottom lip. She had to talk to David this morning. Preferably, just as soon as he was finished with his meeting.

And in the meantime, she had better pray.

Chapter Twelve

David tried to give his full attention to Mark Taylor, who had been damned decent about David's tardiness and who had obviously put a lot of time and thought into his presentation. But no matter how he tried, something niggled at the back of his mind. Something he couldn't banish or figure out.

If you told her how you feel about your job and explained your idea about that boys' ranch to your grandmother, I think she would be proud of you.

That was the gist of what Roxanne had said last night. David frowned again, just as he had then.

How had Roxanne known about his secret ambition? For the life of him, he couldn't remember ever having told her. In fact, he'd taken pains not to reveal this hidden desire, because he was sure she would not approve. Because aside from her father and David's grandmother, Roxanne was the most enthusiastic supporter of David's involvement in the joint family business.

So how had she known about the boys' ranch?

Had someone else told her?

That must be it.

Someone else had told her. But who?

David could count on one hand the number of people he had confided in. In fact, there had been only four. His sociology professor at college. Hank. Andy Simcheck, an older guy he'd worked with and become friends with in Saudi Arabia.

And Rachel.

It was funny about Rachel. He certainly hadn't intended to tell her. It had just seemed to happen.

He smiled, remembering.

It was last Christmas and the two families had spent Christmas Eve together. They'd gone to the candlelight service at their church, then come back to the Carlton house for a late supper. Afterward, they'd sat around the fire with their eggnog and listened to Roxanne play Christmas carols on the piano.

Rachel and David had been sitting together on one of the couches. Rachel had commented about how well Roxanne played.

"She can do so many things well," she'd said.

There'd been a wistfulness in her voice that had touched David, and he thought how much he liked this future sister-in-law of his. He wished she wasn't always selling herself short, though.

"You're talented, too," he told her. "Just in different ways."

She smiled and nodded, but the tinge of sadness remained. "Oh, I know. I'm a good teacher and hopefully a good artist, but...Roxanne is just *different.* She has so many talents. In so many directions. She could be successful at anything she wanted. Take music, for instance. If she'd wanted to, she could have had a performing career. Her teachers all said so." Her smile turned wry. "Nobody ever told *me* that, and I had the same amount of lessons."

"Yeah, but she's not an artist, and *you* are," David observed.

Rachel sighed. "I know. I'm probably not explaining myself well. I guess what I'm trying to say is, Roxanne is one of those really lucky people who has so much ability, she can have just about anything she wants. It's simply a matter of setting her sights on a goal and working toward it. The rest of us, well, some things are attainable by hard work, but mostly we wish for things we haven't a prayer of getting."

"What is it you want that you haven't gotten?"

She didn't answer for a long time. Then, giving herself a little shake, she laughed. "Oh, nothing. I'm just being silly. It's this whole Christmas thing. It always gets to me."

He almost accepted that. Almost went along with her pretense that her earlier comment hadn't been important. But something wouldn't let him. Something told him she needed to know that everyone had secret yearnings, that no one's life—no matter how it appeared on the surface—was perfect.

So he said, "You know, you're right about one thing. Most of us do have secret dreams that are probably not ever going to come true. I'll bet even Roxanne does."

She turned to look at him then, and her blue eyes, so incredibly like Roxanne's, studied him thoughtfully. "You, David?" she said softly. "Do you have secret dreams?"

He smiled wryly. "Sure. I'm not immune." And then, surprising himself, he blurted everything out, telling her about the idea he had for a boys' ranch.

When he finished, her eyes were shining. "Oh, David, it sounds *wonderful.* Why *can't* you do it?"

"You know why." He inclined his head in the direction of his grandmother and her father, who were sitting in matching fireside chairs about a dozen feet away.

As she had since they were kids, Rachel understood without further explanation. That ability to intuit another's feelings so easily had always been one of her finest qualities, David thought.

Yes, he decided now, Rachel must have been the one to tell Roxanne. After all, he hadn't told her to keep it confidential. Rachel wouldn't have felt she was doing anything wrong in discussing the topic. In fact, she would most likely have assumed he'd already confided in her sister.

What surprised him, though, was Roxanne's attitude—that she thought he should tell his grandmother how he felt about his job and what he really wanted to do with his life. In fact, he couldn't believe she was in favor of his idea.

And she must be.

Otherwise, she'd have been trying to talk him out of it last night.

He guessed it was true what everyone said—that you never really knew anyone until you were married to them. He sure as hell hadn't known Roxanne. Why, every day she surprised him by revealing new facets to her personality. And instead of the new facets irritating or disappointing him, they were all pleasant surprises.

You are one lucky son of a gun.

He had the perfect wife, and every day he loved her more. She was the brightest spot in his world, and he couldn't imagine living without her.

He thought about their lovemaking the night before. Although she'd seemed a little reluctant at first—probably because she thought he was too tired—she had quickly become just as eager, just as passionate, and just as responsive as he could ever wish.

He almost laughed as he remembered how—before they were married—he'd worried about that aspect of their relationship.

"Er, Mr. Hanson?"

David almost jumped. He'd been so lost in his thoughts he'd completely forgotten Mark Taylor's existence. Taylor's green eyes seemed amused as David stumbled through an apology, saying, "I'm sorry. I worked late last night and didn't get much sleep. What were you saying?"

"I said we could have the security system in place next Friday, if that's agreeable to you."

For the next fifteen minutes David forced himself to pay attention and put his wife and his feelings for her out of his thoughts. But after Taylor was gone and David sat leafing through the contract he'd left, he resolved that he would reintroduce the subject of the boys' ranch when he got home tonight.

For the first time, David felt a stirring of hope. If Roxanne was really in favor of his leaving the family business, maybe there *was* some way to accomplish it.

Rachel showered and dressed in record time. Again she took special care with her appearance. She wanted to look pretty but not frivolous, so she settled on a black linen sleeveless dress with three rows of decorative white piping around the hemline and neckline. Pearl stud earrings, black-and-white spectator pumps and a soft black leather handbag completed her costume.

She left her hair in its natural, curly state, knowing David liked it best that way.

Before leaving the house, she caught sight of herself in the large mirror in the entryway. A well-dressed, attractive woman with scared-rabbit eyes looked back at her.

Condemned woman walking, she thought grimly.

With a heavy heart, she headed out the door.

David swore under his breath and hung up the phone. No answer. Roxanne had obviously gone out, and she hadn't turned on the answering machine before she'd left the house. Well, there was no help for it. He'd just have to call her later, from Beaumont, where he was going to talk to John Vrable, a possible witness in a case where a former Hanson Drilling employee who had been fired had brought suit against the company. Normally, company attorneys would take care of something like this, but Vrable had refused to talk to anyone unless David was there.

David checked his briefcase to make sure he had everything he needed, then he gave his secretary some last-minute instructions, ending with "And if Roxanne calls, tell her I'll try to get back by seven."

"Will do," Carole said.

Five minutes later, accompanied by their in-house lawyer, he was on his way.

"He's not here?" Rachel said.

"No, Mrs. Hanson, I'm sorry. He and Pete Shearer went to Beaumont to interview John Vrable. You know, in that Bobby Turner case."

Rachel nodded. David had told her all about the case when they were in Colombé.

"I'm sorry," Carole said again.

Rachel tried not to look as if David's not being there was the end of the world, but that's the way she felt.

Now what?

David would be gone all day. He'd try to be back by seven, he'd said. But what if he wasn't? And what if, in the meantime, Roxanne called their father?

Oh, God.

Their father.

Rachel had promised to call him this morning and give him the Terrazas' number in Veracruz. Maybe she should go up to his office now and tell him "Rachel" wasn't going to be home today and would instead call him tomorrow.

No, she decided upon further thought. She couldn't take a chance on seeing her father face-to-face. Not today. In her nerve-racked state of mind, it was just too risky. Instead, she took the elevator down to the lobby and headed for the bank of pay phones.

Pilar put her through immediately.

"Hi, Daddy," Rachel said when her father got on the line. "Just wanted you to know I spoke to Ro...Rachel last night."

Oh, my God. I nearly said Roxanne!

"Good," her father said. "Did you tell her I want to talk to her?"

"Yes, but she and Carlos are going to Mexico City today and won't be back until late. She said to tell you she'd call you tomorrow."

Did he hear *that slip?*

Rachel's heart was pounding so hard she was sure he could probably hear it over the phone line.

"All right," her father said. "Guess I can wait another day. How are *you* doin' today, angel? You plannin' to spend the day at the hospital again?"

Oh, thank God, he didn't hear it. "I—I don't know. I guess I'll give David's grandmother a call. See if she needs anything or wants company."

Just then a couple of women walked by, laughing and talking.

"What's all that noise?" her father said.

"Um, I'm out at the mall."

"Oh, okay. Well, I won't keep you, then. You and David plannin' on droppin' by the house this weekend?"

"We...didn't have a chance to talk about the weekend. We overslept this morning, and David had to rush out."

"Well, if you want to come to Sunday dinner, Josie always makes enough for an army."

"Thanks, Daddy. I—I'll let you know."

"Okay, angel. Thanks for lettin' me know about Rachel."

Rachel was a wreck by the time she hung up, and she worried all the way home. So many lies. So many possibilities for disaster. She couldn't stand lying to the people she loved, and wondered what on earth was going to happen after they knew the truth.

She kept thinking she needed to do something, but what else could she do that she hadn't already done?

There was nothing. She had called Roxanne. She had called her father. She had tried to see David. Now all she could do was try to stop worrying and wait.

Easier said than done, she thought later, pacing around David's house in an agony of turmoil. She needed to keep busy. If only she could go to her own place and lose herself in work.

But how could she?

What if David called?

What if Roxanne called?

What if their father called?

After thirty more minutes of imagining dire happenings and possible scenarios, she went into the bedroom, stripped off the clothes she'd chosen so carefully and put on shorts and a T-shirt. Then, quickly, trying not to think about what she was doing, she packed up everything belonging to her.

Belonging to Roxanne, she corrected herself.

Nothing here belonged to her. Not the clothes. Not the furniture. And not the man. She had laid claim to them falsely.

Now it was time to give them back.

The interview wasn't concluded to Shearer's satisfaction until four o'clock. That was good, though, David thought. He could easily make it home by seven. In fact, he might even have time to stop at the office and tell Wylie how everything had gone.

Before leaving Beaumont, David used his cell

phone and dialed his home number. Roxanne picked it up on the second ring.

"Hi," he said, feeling that rush of happiness her voice always produced.

"Hi."

She seemed subdued, and he wondered if something was wrong, but then he remembered. She'd wanted to talk to him about something this morning and had seemed upset that he'd had to leave in such a rush. What an idiot! How could he have forgotten?

"I'm heading home," he said. "I have to stop at the office first, but I should easily make it by seven."

"Okay."

"Don't cook dinner. I want to go to the hospital tonight, and we can eat somewhere afterward." He softened his voice. "Sweetheart, I know I've been neglecting you lately, but we'll have some quiet time together tonight, I promise, and we can talk to your heart's content."

"Oh, David, you haven't been neglect—"

"Yes, I have," he said, cutting her off. "But that's going to change. I love you. I'll see you soon."

I love you.

A tear slipped down Rachel's cheek.

David was so wonderful.

And she was so horrible.

Since they were going against traffic, David and Pete Shearer made good time on Interstate 10 and reached the office a few minutes before six. Thanking Pete for his help, David headed straight for the twentieth floor and Wylie Carlton's office.

The loyal Pilar was still at her desk. She looked up and smiled as David approached.

"Is he in?" David said.

She nodded. "Uh-huh."

David tapped on the half-open door, and at Wylie's booming "Come in," entered the sun-filled corner office.

"How'd it go?" Wylie said, leaning back in his chair.

"Good." David laid his briefcase down and shrugged out of his suit jacket. Then he sat on one of the four black leather chairs that ringed Wylie's massive walnut desk. He had just started telling Wylie about what Vrable had said when Wylie's intercom buzzed.

Wylie frowned and punched the intercom. "I'm busy, Pilar," he started to say, then stopped. His face lit up. "Really? Rachel's on the line? Well, put her through." He reached for the phone. "Pilar says 'my wayward daughter from Mexico' is calling." His smile couldn't have been bigger.

David smiled back. So Rachel had finally decided to call her father. Good. He'd hated the fact that they were estranged, and he knew it bothered Roxanne, too.

"Rachel? Hello? Rachel? Thought you weren't gonna call me until tomorrow. Leastways, that's what Roxanne said when I talked to her earlier."

David looked at his watch. It was twenty after six already, and he'd promised Roxanne he'd be home by seven. He got up. This conversation could take a while. He mouthed a goodbye to Wylie and picked up his briefcase.

Wylie, obviously listening to whatever it was Rachel was saying, waved back. "Your sister already told me. You're married, right?"

"Tell her I said hi," David said.

Wylie frowned. Listened. "Are you pregnant?" he boomed.

David grimaced and walked to the door.

"Dammit, Rachel!" Wylie was saying. "What's wrong with you? Would you just *tell* me whatever it is?"

David reached for the doorknob.

"What? What the hell are you talkin' about? What do you mean, *you're not Rachel?*"

David stopped dead in his tracks.

"Is this some kind of joke?" Wylie said.

David turned around.

Wylie's eyes, shocked and confused, met his. He pressed a button, and suddenly Rachel's voice sounded through the speaker box.

"No, Daddy," she was saying. "It's not a joke. This really is Roxanne, and I'm in Mexico, and I'm married to Carlos."

David's heart felt as if it were going to burst right out of his chest. His mouth dropped open.

"B-but you *can't* be!" Wylie said. "You...you married *David* two weeks ago."

"No, Daddy, I didn't. That was Rachel who married David. Rachel...pretending to be me."

"Rachel!"

Rachel! David stared at the phone.

"Yes," Roxanne continued. "I'm the one who met Carlos at that consulate party. I know it was wrong, but I just couldn't seem to help myself. I fell in love with him, Daddy, and I didn't know what to do. I was so unhappy. Rachel begged me to tell David how I felt, but I was afraid to. I was afraid you'd be mad at me. The wedding was so close and all the plans were made. You were so happy about it. I just couldn't see any way out of it. I thought I had to go through with the wedding."

David stood numbly, her words pummeling him like stones. Roxanne had run away. Not Rachel. Roxanne.

"Then," Roxanne continued, "the day of the wedding, Carlos came to the church. He said he couldn't go home and leave me behind. He asked me to come with him. And...and I suddenly knew I couldn't go through with marrying David. It wouldn't have been right. So, like a coward, I ran out, leaving Rachel to deal with the mess. She...she told me she couldn't do it. She couldn't go out there and tell you and David that I'd run away...so she put on my wedding dress and pretended to be me."

Wylie looked as stunned as David felt. "Why didn't you tell me, David?"

"David!" Roxanne said. "Is David there?"

"Yes, he's here," Wylie said.

"I didn't know," David said. His voice sounded as if it belonged to someone else. "I didn't know."

"Oh, my God," Roxanne said. "You've got me on the speakerphone, don't you? That's why the line sounded so funny. David? Did...didn't Rachel talk to you this morning?"

David swallowed. "No. No, she didn't."

"Oh, God. Oh, David, I'm sorry."

So that was why she had been so troubled.

That was why, even when they were in Colombé, she'd acted as if something was bothering her. God! What a fool he was! Rachel! It was Rachel he'd married. All this time...

Suddenly everything fell into place.

All the little differences in "Roxanne's" behavior. All the "new" facets to her personality.

No wonder she had known about his desire to start the ranch for underprivileged boys. No wonder she'd acted as if she were harboring a secret. No wonder she kept saying there was something she had to tell him.

Of course it was Rachel he'd married.

How could he ever have imagined it was anyone else?

The knowledge reverberated through him.

Rachel.

And Roxanne had married someone else.

Somehow, that realization did not hurt him the way

he might have imagined it would if he'd ever thought about it.

But Rachel's deception.

That was another story.

All this time...she had been *pretending.* Images from their honeymoon flashed through his mind.

Everything she'd said.

Everything she'd done.

All false.

His shock slowly faded. Hurt and anger warred to take its place.

Even though it would be easy to succumb to the pain, David pushed it away. It was bad enough that Wylie knew what had happened, and that—when he got over his shock—he would probably feel sorry for him. There was no way David was going to let him see the extent of the hurt he felt from the betrayal of his daughter.

He clenched his fists, welcoming the anger that coursed through him, anything to chase away the pain.

How could Rachel have done this?

Why had she done this?

He thought about her waiting at home.

"I have to go," he said. His voice didn't sound like his own.

Wylie nodded sympathetically.

"David!" Roxanne said. "Wait. Don't go yet. I—I want to talk to you."

"I'll talk to you later," David said. "Right now I've got other business to take care of."

Then he swung on his heel and stalked out of the office.

Chapter Thirteen

After David called, Rachel loaded all of Roxanne's belongings—as well as the few of her own that she'd brought to David's—into Roxanne's car.

Then she waited, trying to keep calm as the mantel clock ticked the seconds away.

Five o'clock.

Five-twenty.

Five forty-five.

Because she had to do something, she tried practicing what she would say when he got there. How she would start explaining.

She couldn't just blurt it out.

Oh, by the way, David, guess what? I'm not really Roxanne. I'm Rachel.

Oh, God. She put her head in her hands.

What *was* she going to say? How do you tell someone the person he loves isn't really that person at all? That everything he believes in is a hoax? That both his marriage and his wife are a sham?

Maybe she should start out by saying she wanted to tell him a story. Relate the events as if they had happened to someone else.

No, that was cowardly, and she'd been enough of a coward. It was time to stand tall. Be brave. Face the music. "Oh, just *listen* to me!" she said despairingly. "I sound like every bad cliché in the book."

She glanced at the mantel again and again.

Six-ten.

Could those hands move any more slowly?

Six-twenty.

Six-thirty.

With each tick, Rachel's heart beat harder and her stomach felt more unsettled. She wanted it to be seven o'clock. She wanted this horrible confession to be over with. She wanted whatever was going to happen, to happen.

Walking to the front window, she looked out. It was a typical summer evening in David's active neighborhood. A twenty-something woman whizzed by on a ten-speed. Across the street, two young children played with a terrier in their front yard. Next door to them was a fortyish couple doing yard work. Down the street, a young man washed his car.

Everywhere she looked, people were going on with

their lives, doing ordinary things in ordinary ways, not knowing or caring that here, in this house, Rachel's life was falling apart around her.

Six thirty-five.

She took several deep breaths. *Calm, try to stay calm.* Very soon now she would hear his car in the driveway.

Slowly she turned away from the window, and her gaze traveled over the living room. Although she was unsure about many things, she was certain about one. This was the last time she would be here.

The very last time.

Fighting tears, she looked at each object and each piece of furniture, committing it to memory so that years from now, when the heartache had faded and she could stand thinking again, she could look back and remember this place and time with David.

Everything belonging to him was dear to her.

The stack of *National Geographics* on the bottom shelf of the bookcase. The gold nugget paperweight David had brought back from Saudi Arabia. The silver-framed photograph of his parents—looking so young and blissfully happy—on their wedding day. His favorite pillow. The new James Lee Burke novel he hadn't yet started. His favorite leather chair with the indentation where his head always rested.

Oh, David, I'll miss you so....

The strident ring of the telephone startled her. She raced to get it, praying it wasn't David saying he would be later than he'd thought. "Hello?"

"Rach?"

"Roxanne?"

"Yes. Oh, Rach, something awful's happened."

Rachel's heart stopped.

"You didn't talk to David this morning, did you?"

"No, I couldn't. We overslept and he had a meeting and had to race out. I called the Terraza house and left you a message. Didn't you get it?"

"No, I didn't. Carlos and I are still in Mexico City. We're staying overnight."

Rachel held her breath, terrified of what Roxanne would say next.

"Rachel, I'm so sorry, but I called Daddy. And the worst part is, David was there."

"David was there!"

"Yes. He was in Daddy's office when I called. I didn't know it, but Daddy put me on the speaker-phone, and David heard the conversation."

David was there.

David knew.

"I'm so sorry," Roxanne said again. "I feel rotten about this, but Rach, you *told* me it would be okay to call him tonight."

Rachel's mind churned. David knew. He knew! At this very moment he was probably on his way home *...and he knew.*

"Rach? Are you still there?"

"Yes, I—I'm still here."

"Are you okay?"

I'll never be okay again. "Y-yes."

"Sweetie, I'm sorry."

"W-what did he say?"

"David?"

"Yes, David," Rachel whispered.

Roxanne sighed. "Not much. He was obviously stunned. I tried to talk to him, but he cut me off, said he'd talk to me later. Said he had other business to take care of. Then he left."

Rachel's heart pounded. "Oh, God. He's on his way home. I know it. He'll probably be here any minute. I—I've got to go."

"Wait, Rach. What are you going to do?"

"I don't know. I can't talk now, Roxanne!"

"All right, sweetie, but call me later, okay?" Roxanne said in an agonized voice.

Rachel's hands were trembling so hard, she could barely get the phone back in its cradle. Dear God. Why? Why had this had to happen this way?

How David must hate her.

If only she'd had a chance to break the news gently. To say the things she had wanted to say before actually telling him who she was.

But now...now it was too late.

Now he knew.

What must he be thinking?

The minutes crawled by as her thoughts spun in wild circles. Suddenly she could stand it no longer. She knew it was cowardly, but she just couldn't face David. Not like this. Not now that he knew.

Grabbing the notepad from the kitchen counter, she scribbled a hasty note.

Dear David, I am so sorry you found out the truth the way you did. I tried to tell you last night and again this morning. Please believe me when I say I intended to tell you tonight, no matter what. I know how you must hate me, so I'll make it easy for you by leaving.

She stared at what she had written. It seemed so inadequate. But what else could she say? She thought about ending the note with "I love you," but decided against it. She was sure David didn't care. Besides, he probably wouldn't believe her. After all, she had been lying to him and everyone else for weeks. In fact, the entire note was probably a waste of time. He would probably wad it up and throw it away without believing a single word.

Sick at heart, she simply said she was sorry again and signed her name. After anchoring the note with the saltshaker in the middle of the kitchen table where he'd be sure to see it first thing, she grabbed her purse and hurried out to the driveway.

She nearly flooded the car trying to get it started. But finally the ignition caught and she backed out, narrowly missing a car parked in front of the house next door. She drove down the street as fast as she dared.

A few minutes later, as she waited at the corner for

oncoming traffic to clear so she could turn right onto Buffalo Speedway, she saw David pull in to the left turning lane in preparation for entering the neighborhood. He was looking up at the light and didn't see her. For a moment she stared at his beloved face.

Then, with tears streaming down her cheeks, she accelerated, pulled out into traffic and drove away.

David's head whipped around.

That looked like Roxanne's car!

But by the time he realized it, he'd already turned onto his street and Rachel—if that's who it had been—was gone. A few minutes later he pulled in to his driveway. Sure enough, Roxanne's Mercedes wasn't there.

He had calmed down a lot since leaving the office, because it hadn't taken him long to realize that the Rachel he had known for most of his life could not have done what she'd done without a damned good reason. She certainly would never intentionally do anything to hurt anyone. But he still couldn't figure out *why* she'd done it.

He had to talk to her.

He had to find out why.

Frustrated by her absence, he looked up the street. Why had she left? She knew he would be home soon.

Maybe she knows about Roxanne's phone call.

No. How could she?

Maybe Roxanne called her.

Damn. He hoped not. He hoped the reason Rachel was gone was an errand she'd forgotten to take care of. That was it, he assured himself. She was running an errand and would probably be back in a few minutes.

But then he walked into the kitchen and saw the note, and he knew she hadn't just gone out to run a last-minute errand. With a sinking feeling, he picked up the note and read it.

Gone.

She was gone.

The note slipped from his fingers. He stared into space. Thought about what she'd said…and what she hadn't said.

It was only then that he realized the truth. No wonder he hadn't felt hurt by Roxanne's defection. He didn't love Roxanne. Maybe he never really had.

He loved Rachel.

And he didn't want to lose her.

Rachel cried all the way to her town house. She cried the whole time she unloaded Roxanne's belongings and put them away. She cried as she loaded her own clothing and painting equipment into her minivan. She was still crying fifteen minutes later when she entered the on-ramp to Interstate 10 west.

She wasn't sure she would ever stop.

Where had she gone?

David could think of only two possible places. The town house. Or her father's house. He would try the town house first.

Driving faster than was sensible, he pulled up in front of her town house a scant fifteen minutes later. Because the garage was in the back and contained no windows, there was no point in his going around to see if either of the cars was there. Instead, he walked up the front walk and rang the doorbell. No one answered. He rang again. Still no answer. He pounded on the door. "Rachel," he called, "open up if you're in there."

When he got no response, he walked across the lawn to the front window and peered inside. There were no lights on and no movement.

She wasn't there.

David walked back to his car and got out his cell phone. First he called the office to see if Wylie was still there. The night security guard answered the phone.

"Sorry, Mr. Hanson, they've all gone home."

"Thanks, Marty."

Next David punched in the number of the Carlton house. It rang several times before Josie, the housekeeper, answered. "I'm sorry, Mr. David. Mr. Carlton isn't home yet."

"Oh, okay. Uh, Josie? Is...um, Roxanne there by any chance?" David had almost said "Rachel," then realized that Josie would not know what he was talking about if he did.

"No, Mr. David, she's not. Is she supposed to be?"

"No, I just thought she might have stopped there.

Listen, Josie, if she does happen to come, would you call me?"

"Well, sure," she said, sounding confused. "But wouldn't you rather just have me tell *her* to call you?"

"Well, we, uh, kind of had a fight, and I'm not sure she *would* call me."

Josie chuckled. "I see. A lovers' quarrel. Okay, Mr. David, give me your number. I'll call you if I see her."

"You're a doll, Josie. Thanks."

David sat in his car for a few minutes, trying to think if there was anyone else he could try. He couldn't imagine that Rachel would go to any of her friends' houses. That would entail explaining everything, and he didn't think she'd want to do that. He wondered if maybe she'd just checked in to a hotel, and even entertained the idea of calling around to try to find her. He quickly discarded it. There were hundreds of different hotels and motor hotels in Houston. And he didn't even know if Rachel would use her own name. No, that idea wasn't very practical.

Maybe he should just go home. That way, if she called, he would be there.

When he arrived home, Wylie's car was parked in front of the house and Wylie was leaning against it. "I was just tryin' to decide whether to wait awhile and see if you came home or go home myself," he said, walking down the driveway to meet David. He looked around. "Where's Rachel?"

"I don't know," David said. "When I got here, she was gone." He explained about the note. "I just went over to the town house, but she's not there. And I called at your house, but Josie said she hasn't seen her.''

Wylie frowned.

''Do you have any idea where she might have gone?'' David asked.

Wylie shook his head. ''Maybe to one of her friends'?''

David explained why he thought that was unlikely.

''You're right,'' Wylie said. His frown deepened, and his eyes were worried. ''Maybe I should go home. She might try to call me.''

''That's a good idea.''

''How about you, David? You doin' okay?''

''Yeah, I'm okay.''

Wylie laid his hand on David's shoulder. ''I'm sorry, son. I know this was a rotten thing my girls did to you. And I told Roxanne that. She feels real bad about it.''

David nodded.

''And I'm thinkin' Rachel feels pretty bad, too. Else why would she take off like this?''

Did she? David wondered. He wanted to think she felt bad. He wanted to think she cared about him. He wanted to think that everything she'd said and done hadn't simply been part of the pretense.

''Well, if you talk to Rachel, you tell her to call me.''

''I will.''

Wylie left, and David walked into the house. The

first thing he saw was his answering machine blinking. Rachel! he thought, his heart soaring.

But it wasn't Rachel who had called. It was Roxanne. "Please call me, David, no matter what time you get back," her message said.

It took a while for the call to Veracruz to get through. But finally Roxanne was on the line.

"David? Thank you for calling. I was afraid you might not."

"Yeah, well..."

"I'm so sorry about everything. I wouldn't blame you if you never wanted to talk to me again."

He sighed heavily. "I'm not mad at you."

"You're not?"

"No. I was. I was mad as hell. But I'm not anymore."

"Oh, David. You're such a nice man. I really don't deserve to have you not be mad." She hesitated. "What about Rachel? Are you mad at her?"

"No," he said slowly. "No. I just want to find her."

"Find her? What do you mean?"

"She's gone. She wasn't here when I got home."

"B-but where *is* she?"

"I don't know. She left me a note." He described its contents. "Anyway, she's not at the town house or your father's house and I don't know where else to look."

"Oh, dear. I was afraid of this. She was so upset when I called her."

"So you *did* call her."

"Yes. Well...I *had* to warn her, David. I mean, I thought you were furious, and I didn't want her to be blindsided."

"Yeah. I guess. Still, I wish you hadn't." If Roxanne hadn't called Rachel, maybe he and Rachel would have settled everything by now. Maybe David would know why Rachel had continued to pretend to be Roxanne. Maybe he'd know if there was hope.

"David?"

"What?"

"How...how do you feel about Rachel?"

He thought about saying it was none of Roxanne's business. He thought about lying. He thought about how stupid he would feel if it turned out Rachel felt nothing for him. "I love her," he said quietly.

"Oh, I'm so glad," she said. "You and me, we were never right for each other, but you and Rachel, you're perfect."

"Yes," he said. "We are."

He only hoped he hadn't realized it too late.

Driving nonstop, Rachel reached her father's cabin in the countryside near Wimberley a little after ten-thirty that night. When she'd finally unloaded all of her supplies, it was nearly eleven and she was so exhausted she wasn't sure she had the strength left to undress, so she didn't. She sank onto the couch and closed her eyes.

But two hours later she faced the fact that she

wasn't going to be able to sleep. She just couldn't shut her mind down. She kept imagining David walking into the house and seeing her note. She pictured his face when he read it. Imagined what his thoughts were.

Finally, about two o'clock, she got up and put some water on to boil for tea. When it was ready, she fixed herself a cup and walked outside. She sat on the moonlit porch and sipped her tea and listened to the comforting sounds of crickets chirping and mockingbirds singing and small creatures rustling around in the underbrush.

She thought about everything, from the moment she'd put on Roxanne's wedding dress to the moment she wrote David the goodbye note and left Houston. She thought about how her father had always accused her of having no backbone. Of being a coward. She thought about David and how decent he was and how much she loved him. And she thought about how, in life, we make choices and how, when we make the wrong one, we can ruin our lives.

When, at five-thirty, the first hint of pink crept into the eastern sky, she finally got up and walked inside. Her decision was made. She had run away in a panic, but she couldn't hide out forever. Sooner or later she had to face both David and her father.

It took her only twenty minutes to carry everything she'd brought back out to her car.

By six o'clock she was on her way back home.

At exactly eight minutes after nine Rachel pulled in to the driveway of her father's house. Telling herself she would stay calm no matter how her father ranted at her, she walked up the back steps and rapped softly on the back door.

Josie's wide-eyed face greeted her. "Good morning, Miss Rachel."

So Josie knew. "Good morning, Josie. Is my father here?"

"He's in the dining room, havin' his breakfast. You just go on in."

Rachel nodded. Despite her earlier admonition to stay calm, her heart was beating too fast when she entered the dining room.

Her father lowered the morning paper.

Blue eyes met blue eyes.

What Rachel wanted to do was look away. What she did was inch her chin up a notch higher and meet her father's gaze levelly.

"Well, don't just stand there," he finally said, his voice gruff. "Come on in and sit down."

After first going to the antique sideboard and pouring herself a cup of coffee, Rachel did as he'd instructed. Once she was seated, he said, "I think I understand why you pretended to be Roxanne at the wedding ceremony. What I don't understand is why you didn't just tell me and David the truth afterward."

"I know I should have. But I couldn't do it at the reception, and afterward..." She explained how she'd been thwarted by the attendants hopping into the limo with them and how they'd stayed at the airport until she and David boarded the plane for Miami.

"Why didn't you tell David then?"

If her father had yelled at her, the way she'd expected him to, it would have been harder to admit the truth. But he hadn't. And his eyes were kind. Kind and understanding. More so than she'd ever seen them, at least when they were trained upon her.

Taking a fortifying sip of coffee, she said quietly, "I didn't tell him because I love him, Daddy. I've been in love with him for years." Once she'd admitted that, it became much easier to continue, and soon the whole story spilled out. When she'd finished, she looked at her father anxiously. What was he thinking?

And then he smiled. A big smile. "Little girl, what you did took guts. And comin' here, tellin' me, that took even more."

Tears filled Rachel's eyes. "Oh, Daddy!"

Wylie's eyes looked suspiciously bright, too. He opened his arms. "Come here, darlin'."

Later, after Rachel had cried a little and they'd hugged and kissed and Rachel was once more sitting down with a fresh cup of coffee and the croissant and fresh strawberries Josie had brought her, Wylie said, "So you love David, huh?"

"Yes, Daddy, I do. Very much."

"Then why don't you go to his house and tell him?"

"He doesn't love me," Rachel said sadly. "He loves Roxanne."

"Well, he sure didn't sound like he did when I saw him last night."

"He didn't?"

"Nope. In fact, he sounded pretty frantic to find *you.*"

"Yes, but maybe that's just because he wants to tell me what he thinks of me."

"I don't think so."

Oh, if only her father was right. Still, what did she have to lose? She had intended to go to see David, anyway, to apologize and beg his forgiveness. Why not go all the way and tell him how she really felt?

David hadn't slept much. And when he had, he'd dreamed of Rachel. When he awakened, at six, he was filled with remorse. What had happened had been partially his fault. If he hadn't been so blind and so stupid, he would have realized long ago who he was *really* married to. Well, not really married, he corrected himself. Not legally, anyway.

Still, he should have known. Anyone with any sense would have known that people do not change the way he'd imagined Roxanne had changed.

Desultorily, he fixed coffee, showered and dressed for the day. While he drank his coffee he tried to decide what to do. Should he go out looking for Rachel again?

Or should he just stay put?

Wait...and hope?

* * *

It was ten-thirty before Rachel, heart filled with equal measures of fear and hope, pulled in to David's driveway.

He didn't hear her come in.

She stood in the kitchen doorway and watched him. He was sitting dejectedly, holding a picture of the two of them sitting at a table at their favorite outdoor restaurant in Colombé. Eyes filling with tears, she remembered how she'd felt when the photographer had snapped the picture.

"David?" she said softly.

His head jerked up. "Rachel?" He stood, knocking his chair over behind him. "Rachel!"

It took her only a few seconds to realize he wasn't angry and he didn't hate her. That the look in his eyes was loving and welcoming. With a glad cry, she rushed into his open arms.

"Rachel, Rachel, my love..."

His kiss was urgent, desperate even, and in that moment she knew everything was going to be all right. When he finally raised his head, she saw all the things she had ever wanted to see reflected in his eyes.

"I was afraid I'd never see you again," he said, holding her as if he'd never let her go.

"And I was afraid to face you."

He smiled down into her eyes. "I love you, Rachel."

"Oh, David. And I love you! That's always been true."

"When I got here, and you weren't here, I just about went crazy."

"I'm sorry. I shouldn't have left. But I was so scared. Knowing what I'd done to you, I was sure you hated me. I couldn't stand the thought of seeing that hate in your face."

"Aw, sweetheart, I could never hate you." Then he smiled. "But I was sure mad for a while."

Rachel grimaced.

"That was a dirty trick you and your sister played on me," he said sternly.

"I know. Believe me, I know. I've been agonizing over it for weeks." Guilt assailed her again. She touched his cheek. "I never meant to hurt you, David."

"I know that."

"When did you stop being mad?"

His eyes took on a familiar gleam. "When I remembered all those days...and nights...in Colombé."

Rachel remembered them, too. Suddenly, looking into David's eyes, she couldn't think of anything else.

"I knew you couldn't have been pretending then," he said gruffly. "And if you weren't pretending then, there had to be a reason. I began to hope the reason was because you really loved me as I'd finally realized I loved you."

At his words, Rachel's heart soared. They chased away all the fear, all the unhappiness, and all the empty places that had been in her heart for so long.

After another long kiss, he said, "C'mon, let's go

sit down." Taking her hand, he led her into the living room.

After that, they talked for a long time. Rachel told him everything. How she'd loved him since she was a child. How she'd felt when she'd come home from Paris and discovered that he and Roxanne were practically engaged. And then she told him about the weeks leading up to the wedding. For the most part, he listened quietly, only injecting an occasional question.

When she got to the day of the wedding, it was harder, because her emotions had been so turbulent and her reasoning so clouded, and Rachel wanted to be truthful. For the rest of her life, she wanted to be truthful.

When she finally finished, he said, "I think I always knew, somewhere down deep, that it was you I'd married."

She touched his cheek. Smiled up at him. "We're not really married, you know."

"We can take care of that easily," he said with an answering smile. "Hey, if we have a second ceremony..." He winked. "We'll have to have a second honeymoon."

Rachel chuckled and snuggled closer. As far as she was concerned, if David loved her, the rest of her life would be a honeymoon.

Epilogue

Three months later

"Oh, Rachel, the show is wonderful. And your paintings! They're *fabulous.* Aren't they fabulous, Carlos?"

"Yes, my darling, they are." Carlos, dark eyes amused and loving, smiled down at Roxanne. "And I have already claimed two for our home in London and one for my parents' home in Veracruz."

"That's more than we'll have," David complained good-naturedly, putting his arm around Rachel's waist. "Every time I wanted to keep one, this wife of mine said it had to be in the show."

Rachel grinned at her husband and sister and brother-in-law. The Blythe show was a resounding success. The critics had praised her work, and more than two-thirds of the exhibited paintings were already sold—some for such hefty prices it had made her head swim. She still couldn't believe anyone would be willing to pay so much money for her work. "Hey, we about-to-be-famous artists don't give our work away. If you want one of these paintings so badly, you'll have to buy it," she teased, giving David a nudge.

David made a face. "See what I have to put up with? She's getting bossier every day."

"Good," Roxanne said. "Glad to hear it. We expectant mothers are supposed to be bossy."

Carlos and David exchanged a look.

Roxanne laughed and winked at Rachel.

Rachel thought that if she were any happier, she might burst. Of course, right now, that would be a bad idea, since her daughter wasn't scheduled to be born for another six months. Thinking about the baby she was carrying, she touched her stomach. Sometimes she still felt like pinching herself.

Her eyes met Roxanne's. Roxanne smiled. "We're having a girl, too," she said softly.

"You *are?*" Rachel squealed.

"Uh-huh. Isn't it great? Our daughters will be just about the same age."

"Oh, oh," David said. "Double trouble."

And then they were all laughing, and Rachel—heart

swelled with love and pride and joy—knew, if she lived to be a hundred, there would never again be a moment as perfect as this.

* * * * *

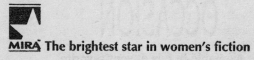

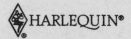

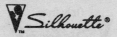

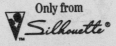